WILD RIDE

a Playing for Keeps novella

CATHRYN FOX

Entangled Publishing, LLC
2614 South Timberline Road
Suite 109
Fort Collins, CO 80525
Visit our website at www.entangledpublishing.com.

Brazen is an imprint of Entangled Publishing, LLC. For more information on our titles, visit www.brazenbooks.com.

Edited by Candace Havens
Cover design by Heather Howland
Cover art from Jenn LeBlanc and Shutterstock

Manufactured in the United States of America

First Edition October 2015

ENTANGLED
BRAZEN

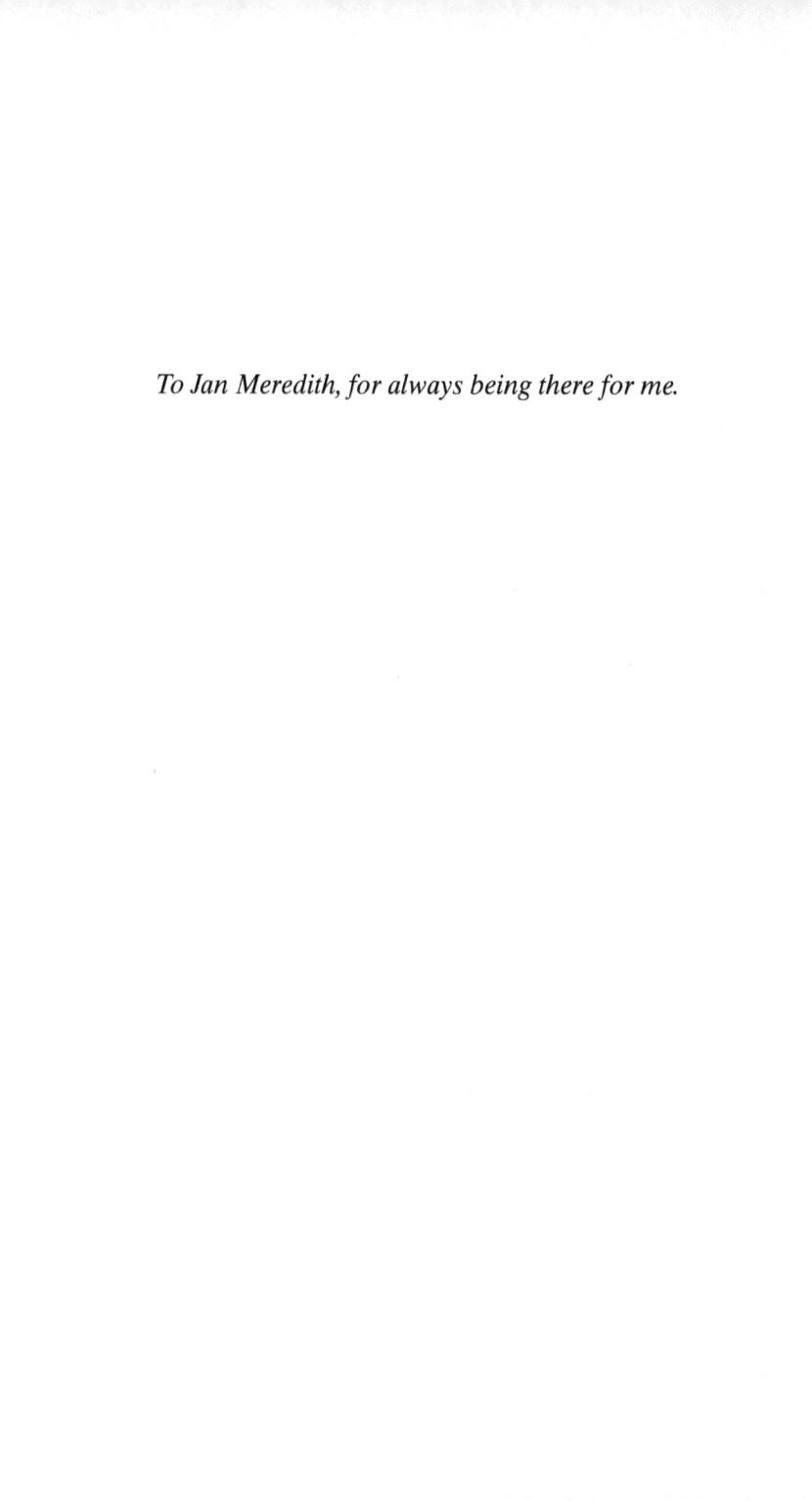

To Jan Meredith, for always being there for me.

Chapter One

Jesus Christ this was a stupid idea. Stupidest goddamn idea he'd ever heard. And as president and owner of Mackenzie Marketing, the East Coast's most successful advertising company, Tyler Mackenzie knew a stupid idea when he heard one. So why the hell had he agreed to it when his best friend Chase Cooper suggested he and their other best friend Curtis Jagger all contact the girls from their past, the ones they thought had gotten away, to see if they could have a future?

Because I'd never gotten over that sweet kiss I shared with her, that's why.

Mac glanced at Coop and Jag as they all stood under a towering oak tree watching the small plane land on the ranch's makeshift runway. The warm afternoon sun broke through the canopy of leaves overhead; Mac fisted his hands and exhaled slowly, but it did nothing to ease the cold knot of apprehension tightening his gut.

Sure he'd thought of Jess Gray over the years, the shy,

quiet girl next door he'd spent his high school years crushing on, the one who'd always listened silently, carefully, when he spoke, but had little to say in return. But having Jag's private investigative company track her down while Mac put together a proposal he'd hoped she couldn't refuse was a damn stupid idea. Shit. When this was all over he'd have to remember to kick Coop's ass.

Tessa Turner, the experienced ranch hand who ran things when the guys were back home in Nova Scotia, where they all held down full-time jobs, met the plane as it came to a stop. The door opened and Mac swallowed against the dryness in his throat as the passengers began to disembark.

Had he mentioned this was a stupid idea?

He shifted his weight from one foot to the other and rolled his shoulders, trying to ease the ball of tension building between them. Honestly, what were the odds that any of the three girls would show, anyway? An anonymous invitation to a working dude ranch in Springvale, Alberta, for a week of R&R would probably come off as a little sketchy to smart, educated women like them. Yeah, he had nothing to worry about. The chance of Jess actually climbing off that plane was slim to none.

Or not.

The second he saw a long set of legs touch the first step he knew it was her. As a yoga instructor, her body was lean and fit, and he'd recognize those sleek legs anywhere. His heart hammered against his ribs, and his knees damn near gave out on him as he waited in anticipation. Jesus, his palms were even sweaty. The world seemed to close in on him as he continued to watch her move down the steps. Off in the distance near the horse corral, he could hear someone calling out to him, but he couldn't make out what they were saying over the sound of his pulse drumming in his ears.

"Holy shit," he murmured, driving his hands into his jeans as he watched her pull her bag tight to her chest, her long dark hair brushing against her shoulders as she glanced around, trying to orient herself.

Jess was here. She was actually here.

Still trying to wrap his brain around the fact that she'd accepted the invitation and boarded the plane, Mac moved toward her on legs not quite steady. She turned curious brown eyes on him and he stopped to remove his Stetson, which shadowed the lower half of his head and neck. She studied him a moment, taking a good long look, then her mouth parted in an *O* of surprise as recognition registered on her face. When their eyes met and held, she gifted him with a smile. A smile so bright and disarming, this time he found his entire body breaking out in a sweat—and it had nothing to do with the scorching sun.

He put his hat back on and looked her over. Taking in the dress she was wearing, and the soft auburn highlights in her hair. Jesus, she'd been pretty back in high school, but now she was...beautiful. Jess Gray had blossomed into a gorgeous woman whom he couldn't wait one more second to get to know better. Strides determined, and with the world around him fading to a dull buzz, he quickly closed the distance between them. His heart thundered in his head as everything about her set off a storm inside him.

But as he approached, her smile fell and panic moved into her eyes. What the hell? Hooves sounded on the dry ground and that's when he realized the thundering wasn't coming from inside his head. She looked over his shoulder and faltered backward, and the next thing Mac knew they were both flat out on the ground, his body pressing hers into the soil. He immediately came up on his elbow and brushed her hair from her forehead, wanting to protect her from his weight bearing down on her. He shifted to the side. "Are you okay?" he asked quickly, unease tightening his gut as his gaze moved to her face. Fuck, if he hurt her…

"I'm okay," she said quietly.

Dust roared up around him, and when something nudged him he turned to see his horse Eleanor.

"Shit," ranch hand Blake Callahan said as he came running over. "Sorry, Mac. She got loose. I tried to warn you but you didn't hear." Blake grabbed Eleanor's harness. "She's been temperamental lately."

"It's okay," Mac assured Blake as the ranch hand started to guide Mac's pregnant mare back to her stall. "She's been a little possessive of me all week."

Blake ran a gentle hand over the horse's protruding side. "She's getting close."

"I'll check on her in a few," Mac promised, watching Blake lead the mare away.

When they were out of sight, he turned his attention back to Jess, and her body softened beneath his as their gazes once again collided. While he wanted to apologize — Christ, he hadn't expected their first meeting after ten years to go down quite like that — he couldn't say he was sorry that Eleanor had gotten loose and knocked him into her.

"You sure you're okay?" he asked again and slipped his hand around her head to lift it off the hard ground and provide a cushiony place for it to rest.

Jess nodded, her cheeks turning a pretty shade of pink.

"I'm okay," she said breathlessly. "You?"

"Yeah. I'm okay." Warm familiarity curled around him and he couldn't seem to move—didn't want to move. He stayed on top of her, his glance moving over her pretty face, her mouth. Lips he'd kissed so long ago, and was dying to kiss again. Jess Gray. Jesus, he couldn't believe she'd actually taken him up on his invitation, or that he had one whole week to spend with her and explore the pull between them, one he felt now, every bit as much as he had all those years ago.

"Mac?" she asked.

He looked deep into her eyes, dark, expressive eyes that told him so much about her. He took a moment to recall that kiss from long ago—one he'd tricked her into—yeah, he was always the joker back in the day. The high school gym had been full of students and teachers, celebrating the last dance before Christmas vacation. He'd called her over to the doorway, and when she reached him, he pointed upward. He remembered the flush on her cheeks, much like the flush she had now, when she saw the mistletoe dangling over his head. She'd opened her mouth to say something and that's when he kissed her. So sweet. So fucking soft and sweet. That kiss, not to mention the journal of hers that he'd managed to get a quick peek at earlier that same day, had told him so much about the girl beneath the shy surface, so much about who Jess really was, and what she truly wanted. But when he'd pulled back she took off, leaving him standing there completely crushed and utterly speechless. Never before, or after, had any woman left him feeling so…confused after a simple kiss.

As he looked her over now, it occurred to him he never wanted to frighten her off like that again. She might be shy and sensitive, bringing out the protector in him, but she also had a quiet strength about her. It was just going to take the right guy to show her she was strong, beautiful, and desirable. The right guy to coax her out from her shell and release her adventurous spirit, one he'd discovered that fateful night so long ago. There was no doubt he wanted to be the guy she needed.

Hell, he *would* be the guy she needed.

He looked at her lips, full, plump...so damn kissable. Her hair splayed across the ground, and a bevy of fantasies rushed through his brain, mainly how she'd look spread out on his bed. He swallowed the groan of want rumbling in his throat.

"What...what am I doing here?" she asked.

He touched a strand of hair, running it though his thumb and forefinger. "I needed to see you."

"You did?" she asked, confused. "Why?"

"Because we have some unfinished business, Jess."

"We do?"

He brushed his thumb over her cheek. "Yeah, we do," he said quietly, completely blown away that she was here, with him. Jesus, he was the luckiest man alive.

She went quiet for a moment, and then she said, "Perhaps we should get up, so you can explain it to me."

Shit, he hadn't even realized they were still on the ground. "Right." He inched upward and frowned when he noticed the dust caking her sundress. "And we should probably get you out of these clothes."

Her eyes dimmed with something akin to desire and Mac couldn't help but smile. This was the best goddamn idea Coop had ever had.

He'd have to remember to thank him when this was all over.

Chapter Two

"You can't be serious."

Jess Gray could hardly believe what she was hearing, what the boy from her past was suggesting. Surely he had to be kidding, playing one of his infamous childhood pranks on her.

Perched at the edge of the ranch's crystal-clear pool, Tyler Mackenzie, aka Wildman Mac, casually rolled to his feet and stretched out his long, athletic body with the same lazy ease Jess remembered from their youth.

There wasn't a hint of teasing in his voice when he answered with, "I've never been more serious in my life."

Jess blinked against the blinding glare of the late afternoon sun reflecting on the water and struggled to wrap her mind around this unexpected turn of events. Exactly when had the invitation for a week of R&R evolved into them getting reacquainted?

Good Lord, she could only imagine what he meant by

reacquainted.

She sucked in a breath, letting the aromatic scent of fresh hay and warm, country air soothe her soul. But the relaxing atmosphere did little to calm her nerves, not when Mac began to undress right before her eyes. Lacking any sort of modesty, he peeled off his T-shirt to expose a gorgeous, muscular torso, one that instantly caught Jess's attention and quite frankly, aroused her.

In a nearby pasture, a stallion whinnied, followed by a chorus of crickets. The sounds caught on a breeze and drifted past them. As she listened to the cacophony of ranch noises, Mac gifted her with a lopsided grin full of sensual promises.

"So, what do you think?" he asked as heat pooled between her thighs. He tipped his Stetson, his eyes full of fierce determination when he added, "Are you up to spending one full week here on the ranch with me…my rules, my terms?"

His rich voice trickled down her spine and elicited a shiver from deep within. It became glaringly apparent that she was no longer staring at the class clown from her childhood, a lawless ruffian known for his practical jokes. No, the Tyler Mackenzie standing before her had grown into a man—tall, gorgeous, hard in all the right places—and while the rebellion from his youth no longer colored his personality, the Mac looking down at her now still had stubborn resolve written all over him. As she entertained his question, shocked that he'd gone to so much trouble to arrange this reunion, it occurred to her that this Mac wasn't quite so different from the one she'd known in high school after all, because when he set his mind to getting what he wanted, he'd go to extreme measures to get it as well.

And this time, he wanted her.

With her voice lodged somewhere in her throat, she didn't answer him. Instead, Jess averted her eyes, lifted her face to the sky, and drank in the sun's warmth as she mulled things over and fought the urge to gawk at his magnificent body. It was a difficult task, considering how badly she wanted to let her hungry gaze trail down the firm ridges of his abdomen, to follow the sexy line of hair that disappeared into the faded jeans that hung low on his hips and did little to hide the huge bulge pressing insistently against the zipper.

Unable to help herself, she stole another peek at him, registering every delicious detail of his fine body as sunlight spilled over him. Awareness soared through her bloodstream as her gaze shifted to his face. She took in his hard angles and noted the way he towered over her, confidence and sex dripping from his every pore as he haphazardly tossed his shirt and hat onto a lounge chair.

Her breasts grew heavy and full, highly sensitive inside her suddenly too-tight demi-bra, the telltale hardening of her nipples letting the world know what the half-naked—half-hard—cowboy was doing to her libido. Jess crossed her arms over her chest to hide her arousal and pinched her thighs together in an effort to get herself under control.

Publicly lusting after a guy was so uncharacteristic of her. Everyone knew she was shy, quiet, and conservative—a good girl who never had the nerve to put herself out there sexually, even though she'd always wanted to. This, of course, was why she kept her naughty fantasies to herself, secretly writing them down in the private journal she kept tucked under her mattress. But there was something about Mac, something from the way he moved with self-assurance to the perceptive way he looked at her, like he could see beneath the surface and read every desire that tempted the vixen inside to come out and play. The truth was, everything about him made her think about sex. Hot. Hard. Toss-me-onto-the-hay-pile kind of sex.

Her mind took that moment to careen in an erotic direction, urging her to step out of character and bring a few of her written fantasies to life. Honest to God, she'd be crazy not to, considering the boy from her youth had grown into a drool-worthy cowboy, one she'd likely never see after this week. She had no doubt getting *reacquainted* was a euphemism for sex, and when it came right down to it, wasn't he presenting her with the perfect opportunity to break free and indulge? She knew Mac, trusted him...well, she trusted the boy she remembered from her youth, anyway. So why the heck shouldn't she spend the week bedded down with him? Mac was just the guy to help her play out her fantasies and take her beyond her wildest imagination.

Jess sucked in a quick breath, both shocked and excited at the direction of her thoughts. She panned the wide expanse of ranch and took in the corrals, the horses, the man-made lake off in the distance, the lodge that sat in the shadows of the towering Rocky Mountains, and the large homestead near the lodge that looked empty.

A week ago, she never would have expected to find herself smack-dab in the middle of a working dude ranch, thousands of miles away from home. But when the anonymous invitation had arrived by courier and promised a week of rest and relaxation at an all-inclusive ranch in Springvale, Alberta—a far cry from her beloved one-bedroom condo and yoga studio on Canada's East Coast—she couldn't help but be intrigued. Nor could she help but think there was a mix-up of sorts. She didn't know anyone out west, or even outside Nova Scotia, for that matter. But after a bit of research, she discovered the invitation was legitimate. She went to the airport out of curiosity, and when she recognized two women from her high school days and they all exchanged similar stories, the next thing she knew, the three of them were boarding the plane to embark on a cross-country adventure.

The last thing she expected to find was Mac and his proposal waiting on the other side for her.

"So, let me get this straight. You invite me to this ranch. A ranch you own with Coop and Jag," she clarified, waving a finger toward the lodge, where she saw Mac's childhood best friends enter earlier. "Because you want me to spend one week with you so we can get reacquainted, because we have unfinished business?"

"I've never been able to get you out of my head, Jess," Mac said honestly. His glance met hers, his eyes so piercing and serious her heart missed a beat. "No matter how many women I've kissed over the years, your lips are the ones that still haunt me." He stood there staring at her waiting for her to say something. "I need to know, Jess. I need to see this thing"—he stopped and waved a finger back and forth between them—"this connection between us through. If I don't, I'll regret it for the rest of my life."

Butterflies took flight in her stomach, as she thought about how they could go about that. "Then why your rules, your terms?" she asked.

He angled his head, his eyes moving slowly over her face. "Do you still trust me?"

"Yes," she said, without hesitation, realizing he'd never

done anything to break the trust they had in their youth.

"Okay, then I need you to trust me on this. By the end of the week, you'll understand."

She nodded, and as she thought things over, he turned his attention to his boots. He toed them off and reached for his belt buckle.

Good God, he's not about to strip down naked in front of me, is he?

The snap of his jeans coupled with the hiss of his zipper answered her question. Jess broke out in a sweat as he pulled off his jeans and stood before her in nothing but his boxer briefs. A tortured noise crawled out of her throat, and she hoped like hell he hadn't heard it. She squirmed restlessly on the edge of the pool, then kicked off her sensible shoes to dip her feet into the frigid water, praying it would help cool down her libidinous body, or at least one spot in particular.

Fully aware that she was gazing at the hottest guy she'd ever known, Jess briefly closed her eyes and worked to settle her rattled nerves. When her lashes flickered open, Mac turned his back to her, giving her an up-close-and-personal view of his ass before diving headfirst into the deep end. Cold waves splashed up to soak the dusty sundress she'd yet to change out of, and the droplets practically sizzled when they landed on her scorching flesh. He disappeared under the water, and she took a moment, her mind reeling, trying to make sense of what was happening.

Mac wants to explore the connection between us.

A connection he'd tried to explore all those years ago, but she'd never given him the chance. She recalled the stolen kiss under the mistletoe during their high school Christmas dance. And oh what a kiss it was.

When they were younger, Mac and his mother had often visited her house. As an introvert herself, and an only child, she would always listen intently when they were alone and Mac shared his dreams. But years later, when out with his friends, he was loud and boisterous, always on the quest for the next exhilarating adventure. He was a force to be reckoned with and rarely stayed in a relationship for long—his antics between the sheets were as legendary as his practical jokes.

Even though his outgoing personality always scared her off in high school, it made him into a successful marketing tycoon. Not only had she read about him in the papers over the years, a workaholic who flew around the country making business deals, but his towering office complex was just around the corner from her yoga studio.

"Why did you bring me *here* for this, Mac?" she asked.

Standing waist-deep in the water, he waved a hand around the vast land. "Out here in the middle of nowhere, with nothing to distract us, it's the perfect place to spend some quality time together, don't you think?" He went quiet for a moment, thoughtful, then added, "Remember when we were kids, and it was just the two of us?"

"Yeah," she said, her heart warming at the memories.

The hard angles of his face softened, making him look so adorable when he said, "I miss those times, Jess. I miss you."

Beneath the blue in his eyes, she caught a glimpse of something deeper, something that made her think that maybe, just maybe, this arrangement wasn't all about sex. She quickly dismissed that thought, reminding herself this was Wildman Mac she was talking about, and since he was trouble with a capital *T*, he'd probably had the horse knock him into her on purpose.

He pushed off from the pool wall and swam toward her. Every nerve in her body came alive, and despite everything, she couldn't deny that she was interested to hear more. His head came up by her knees and he propped himself on the ledge, his arms draped over her thighs as he shimmied in close and pulled himself up until his lips were inches from hers.

His gaze moved over her face before settling on her mouth. Jess drew her bottom lip between her teeth. Was he going to kiss her? Conscious of the way he was studying her, his penetrating blue eyes gauging her reaction to his closeness, she shifted restlessly, but he pressed down on her, preventing her from escaping his intimate hold.

Her entire body felt hot, her nipples achingly hard when she lowered her eyes. His close proximity and scent were doing delicious things to her senses. Even though she'd written out a few explicit fantasies in her private journal, ones that shocked her and left her quivering with need, Jess had never experienced such lust before, her body craving something far naughtier from this sexy cowboy.

Did she dare?

"Is what you have in mind legal?" she asked, trying not to sound as breathless as she felt. She cocked her head, giving him a knowing smile.

His lopsided grin turned her inside out. "I've never done anything illegal in my life."

"I was there that day, remember?"

"Okay, okay, so I jacked a licorice when I was ten. But only because I'd already spent my allowance and you really wanted one. I paid it back the next week."

Her eyes widened. "You did? So did I."

With that they laughed. When he gripped her legs, pushing them open, the laughter died. A quick tug, and he pulled her closer to the pool's edge. Bracing his hands on either side of her thighs, Mac hoisted himself higher, aligning her body intimately with his. Her dress rode high on her thighs and she trembled, fully aware that the only thing separating their private parts was her skimpy panties and—her gaze dropped to the waistband of his underwear and then lower—his wet boxers, which showcased his hardness, despite the cold water.

"You want to touch me, Jess?"

Her eyes snapped back to his and then quickly away again, heat staining her cheeks at having been caught checking him out. He rocked against her, once, just hard enough to let her know what she was doing to him, then leaned down, the rough drag of his stubble scraping her cheek as he whispered, "I'll let you. Anywhere, anytime, and anything you want, for as long as you want. As long as I get to do the same to you."

She swallowed, and the corners of his mouth lifted.

He put his finger under her chin and lifted it until their eyes met. Heat rose up and spread across her neck, the prickle heightened by the rasp of his beard. She clasped her hands, wishing she at least had the nerve to brush away the beads of water dripping down his chiseled face.

When she didn't answer, he said, "Nothing to say? Then let me tell you what I want." The pad of his thumb grazed her bottom lip. "This mouth. Like I said, it's haunted me since that kiss." He leaned in, stroked his tongue down the path his thumb had taken. "I've been giving a lot of thought to this mouth. If it's still as soft, still tastes as sweet." His mouth brushed over hers, dragging a tiny sound from her throat. "Ummm, yes," he dragged the word out on a hiss of pleasure.

Heat consumed her, raced through her veins, and settled with a throbbing ache between her thighs.

"One week," he said, his voice deep, rough, intimate. His hand trailed up her thigh, and there was nothing impersonal in the way he touched her when he added, "One week to explore this connection between us."

A fine shiver moved through her, and it took a bit of effort to redirect her thoughts. Common sense told her to say no, because everything in the warm, intimate way he looked at her, the things he said to her—Lord, the things he said— warned that she could fall hard for the boy she'd crushed on back in the day. Except she had no doubt that by the end of the week, Wildman Mac, a man always on a quest for excitement, would get bored and move on to someone else.

But there was another part of her, one that was a little curious to know what it would be like to spend a week with him and play out a few of her journal entries. It wasn't like *she* hadn't thought about that kiss over the years, or imagined what it would feel like to have those rugged hands of his on her body, touching her in ways she craved, ways she'd written down but never had the nerve to explore.

The more she thought about it, and well, yes, the way he kept using that scruff on his jaw as a weapon of temptation, the better it sounded. She was a big girl, knew the score. She'd be a fool to pass on an opportunity to have her sexual fantasies acted out by a man who'd played a lead role in them more times than not. As long as she knew what she was getting herself into, was careful not to get too close to a man known for his love 'em and leave 'em playboy ways, she could walk away with her body thrumming from satisfaction and her heart completely intact.

The truth was, with no yoga classes scheduled for the next week because her business was failing, and no man waiting to warm her bed, she had no reason to return back home. She pulled the country air into her lungs, letting it relax her as she warmed to the idea of staying. There was no doubt she could use a break from the stresses at home, and the thoughts of losing her business scared her. She'd worked so hard to start it, and after investing every cent she had, watching it fail would tear her apart.

"What do you say?" he asked as he angled his head and twirled a strand of her hair around his thumb.

The back of his fingers grazed her cheek, and desire stirred within her, urging her to experiment with another side of herself, to put herself in this man's hands. She swallowed and worked to sound casual when she asked, "What are your terms?"

He gave her his infamous bad-boy grin, and need settled deep into her core as his eyes devoured her with heat and hunger. "Let me lead the way, no questions asked."

She sucked in a quick breath and considered what he was saying, what he was asking of her. Honestly, it was so outrageous. So exciting. So utterly tempting.

"What if I don't like where you're leading me?"

His sexy grin widened. "You will."

"But what if I *don't*?"

"All you have to do is say stop." His eyes held hers, full of promise and sincerity. "If you'll trust me, I'll give you a week you'll never forget."

A shiver of heat moved through her as his self-assured, dominating attitude awakened something primal inside her. "Pretty confident, aren't you?"

His eyes flared hot. "Yes."

With him caged between her legs as that one word bounced around inside her head, she thought about the places he could take her, all the deliciously naughty ways Wildman Mac could draw her out of her shell and help her find the courage to do things she'd only ever dreamed of doing.

"Say yes."

She opened her mouth, and while that little voice in her head told her to say no—everything inside her screamed that his proposal was ludicrous, and that she should get on the next plane and go home—there was another part that urged her to kick caution in the ass and say, *farewell my old friend, but you are outta here!* After all, what had her shy and quiet, bore-me-to-tears nature done for her? She was still single and her business was on the brink of bankruptcy. As for her love life? Well, hell. It was bankrupt, too.

"Well?" he asked, and leaned in closer, his body brushing hers in the most provocative ways.

"So I have to do *everything* you ask?"

"Everything," he said. A long pause and then, "Do we have a deal?"

Her heart raced, heat and desire zinging through her bloodstream. Even though she was nervous, completely apprehensive about the whole situation, the ravenous way he was looking at her told her she'd be crazy to turn down such a delicious proposition. After all, when would another one like it ever present itself?

Suddenly excited by the prospect of giving herself over to Mac for one full week and realizing how eager she was to experience something new and to discover what he had in store for her, she fought down the unease and wet her bottom lip.

"You're a very persuasive man," she responded. "It's no wonder you're so good at what you do."

"So does that mean—?"

"Yes."

"I need to hear the words."

"I'll do it," she said, her words tumbling out in a breathless rush. "I'll do everything you ask. No questions."

Mac grinned, reared back, and pulled her into the water. Jess gave a startled yelp as the coolness engulfed her heated flesh, but Mac was there, slipping his arms around her, his big hands splaying over her lower back in a protective way, in a way that told her she had nothing to fear, while his legs worked to keep them afloat.

"Trust me," he said, his first command.

With Mac's breath hot against her skin and his groin pressed against hers, Jess angled her hips, fitting his hardness into the notch of her thighs. Could have been nerves, could have been her brain in overload of sexy wet man pressing closer, but she suddenly found herself nodding in agreement.

"Okay," she said, suddenly very anxious to see where this weekend cowboy planned to take her, just how he intended to prove she was the girl for him. But suddenly, the logical part of her brain kicked in, the part that wondered what the heck her inner vixen had just agreed to.

She was both nervous and excited to find out.

Chapter Three

Mac tugged Jess close, water splashing around them as he anchored her small, lithe body to his. Despite the fact that they were in a cold pool, the heat they generated was enough to boil the water. There was no denying the natural attraction between them—one she'd never given him the chance to act on. When Coop had set this plan into motion, she was the only girl who'd come to mind. Looking at her now, tucked under his arm as if she'd been tailor-made for him, it made him feel alive again, something he hadn't felt in years.

Honestly, she was unlike any woman he'd ever met. She had the body of a dancer, but it wasn't just her outer beauty that attracted him; it was the warmth she exuded, her inner peace and quiet strength, and goddammit, he missed having her in his life.

They'd grown up next door from each other, and while their mothers had been friends, she'd never really opened up to him. When they were kids, she always listened intently when he spoke, but when they got older and his circle of friends grew, he'd always tried to involve her, only for her to whip around and head in the opposite direction. But here on the ranch, with no return flight until tomorrow night, she had nowhere to run. Not that she seemed in a hurry to escape. In fact, she seemed genuinely intrigued by his offer. From the intense way she looked at him to the way her expressive honey-flecked eyes gleamed with desire when he laid out his plan, Mac knew she was interested in exploring so much more.

And explore they would.

That night, all those years ago, when he'd first kissed her, caught words like "ménage" and "kink" in her journal, he knew there was another side to her. Damned if he wasn't going to be the man to help her shed her inhibitions and introduce her to a world of pleasure, giving her everything she ever wanted but never had the courage to ask for.

He dipped his head, felt the rush of her hot breath on his face as her chest rose and fell erratically. She moistened her lips like she was waiting for him to kiss her, and he would, when the time was right. His cock twitched in anticipation and pressed against her stomach. She looked past his shoulders when the sound of voices reached the pool area.

"Jess," he said in a firm tone that brought her attention back to him. He moved against her, letting her know exactly what she did to him, and her eyes widened as he lifted her onto his hips, wrapping her long legs behind his back.

"Someone's coming," she whispered as he pressed her against the pool wall with his chest, caging her there with his arms.

When he heard Blake's voice closing in behind him, he cursed silently and inched back to put a measure of distance between them. This was neither the time nor the place to take her where she needed to go.

"Hey, Mac," Blake called out. "Looks like Eleanor has finally settled down."

Mac cleared his throat. "Glad to hear it," he responded. He turned to see his friend, who was escorting a group of newcomers around the property for their familiarization tour.

Mac pushed farther away from Jess and noticed the way her glance moved over Blake as he stepped up to the pool's edge. Mac felt a flash of possession, but then, because this was about her, he considered the curiosity in Jess's eyes, the flicker of interest as she took in the rough and rugged ranch hand, a guy Mac enjoyed hanging out with, on and off the ranch. Oh yeah, he had no doubt there was another side to the girl from his past, and he was going to do whatever it took to help her discover every facet of her sexuality while he deepened the connection between them.

"You heading to Wranglers tonight?" Blake asked Mac, his gaze moving to Jess.

"No," Mac said.

Blake angled his head and gave Mac a wide smile that spoke volumes. "That's too bad. I guess I'll see you around then." Blake gave Jess one last lingering look, then led the group of guests to the east barn, the same barn where Eleanor was resting.

Jess gave Mac a confused look. "What was that all about? What's Wranglers?"

He swam back to her, pulled her close, and shrugged.

"It's just a club."

Intrigue backlit her expressive dark eyes, and he could almost hear the wheels spinning when she asked in a low, almost seductive voice, "What kind of club?"

He cocked his head, and when he saw the real curiosity moving over her pretty face, he said, "A private club, where private things happen."

"Oh," she said, drawing her bottom lip between her teeth. "So you mean like, a sex club?"

He watched her, reading her body language. "Wait, do you want to go?"

She drew in a breath, her glance momentarily flickering to Blake before he disappeared inside the barn. Turning back to Mac, she said quietly, almost demurely, "I guess that's up to you, since you're the one calling the shots."

Mac couldn't help but laugh. Jesus, he had no doubt that discovering all her desires, all her secret fetishes, as he coaxed her out of her shell was going to be as exciting for him as it was for her. But first he wanted to get to know her better outside the bedroom.

"Come on," he said, jumping from the water and pulling her out with him.

"Where?" she asked as her wet body collided with his.

He groaned and fought down the heat rising in him. "There's someone I want to *formally* introduce you to."

"Oh? And who might that be?" she asked, suspicion in her eyes.

He grabbed his clothes off the pool deck and reached for her hand. "Eleanor."

"Ah, Eleanor. The infamous runaway horse."

He eyed her. "Why is it I get the feeling you think I had

something to do with that?"

"The jury's still out," she replied, and he couldn't help but laugh.

He looked over her wet clothes. "First I should let you get changed. Benjamin delivered your luggage to your room already."

"Benjamin?

"Retired rodeo rider who now works the front desk. You'll love him."

He guided her to the main lodge and noted the way she kept throwing glances his way. "What?" he asked as he slicked his wet hair back.

"I don't know. I guess it just surprises me to find you here in the middle of nowhere." She looked around. "I figured you'd need to be somewhere where there was a constant source of excitement."

"Believe me, there is always something exciting happening around here, and if not…" He paused to give her a wink before adding, "Wrangler's isn't too far away."

He led her into the main lodge, but Benjamin was nowhere to be found. "He probably left your room open for you." They took the stairs to the second level, and he pushed her door open for her.

Jess stepped in and her eyes widened as she took in the king-size bed, the pretty floral bedding, handcrafted oak furniture, and a vase full of fresh flowers that he'd picked earlier that morning, when he'd thought this was a stupid idea.

She stepped up to the dresser and breathed in the bouquet. "Gorgeous," she whispered. Turning, she leaned against the dresser and said, "This whole room is so…so pretty."

"Not what you expected?"

"Let's just say today has been full of surprises." She walked to her bed, where Ben had left her suitcase. She unzipped it and pulled out another dress, knocking what looked like a journal to the floor.

It instantly sent his thoughts careening back in time, to the day he looked over her shoulder to glimpse a few words. Always curious to read more, to understand her needs better, he picked it up and flipped it open.

"Mac, don't," she lunged for it and held it to her chest. Her eyes were wide when she asked, "Did you read anything?"

He dipped his head. "What is it you don't want me to see?"

She drew her bottom lip between her teeth. "Nothing."

"If it's nothing, why can't I see?" She clutched it tighter. "Because…"

"I thought you said you trusted me."

"But it's my…my most private thoughts."

Interested to hear more, he prodded, "As in your private fantasies?" He watched her for a long moment, and then asked, "Do you trust me enough to let me read one? You can pick it out if you'd like."

"I don't think I could do that."

Undeterred, he pressed, "Okay, how about you close your eyes, and open to a page." He stepped closer, and she quivered as he ran his finger down her arm. "We only have a week here, and while I'd like to fulfill every fantasy you have in that journal, we don't have time. If you show me, I could at least be sure to fill one or two." Her hand loosened on the book, and in a soft voice, he commanded, "Show me, Jess."

She blew out a shaky breath. "I can't believe I'm doing

this." Closing her eyes, Jess pulled the book open and handed it to him.

She kept her eyes squeezed shut as Mac quickly read through the passage, his mind racing with ideas as he absorbed her words.

After a moment he said, "You can open your eyes now."

When her lids flickered open, he closed the book and handed it back.

"What did you read?" she asked, nervousness and intrigue in her eyes.

"Time will tell," was all he said, and then he jerked his thumb toward the hall. "My room is beside yours. I'll get changed and be right back."

Mac hurried to his room and pulled on a clean shirt and pair of jeans. He tugged on the collar as he thought about what he'd read. His heart beat a little faster and he raked a shaky hand through his hair, wondering if he'd be able to do that for her. It's not like he hadn't gone there in the past, done those things, but this was Jess...his Jess...and, well, that changed everything for him.

Once dressed, Mac hurried back to find Jess standing in her doorway waiting for him, that pretty pink flush still coloring her cheeks.

"Ready?" he asked.

"As ready as I'll ever be," she said.

"Come on then." He grabbed her hand again and led her to the barn. Her eyes widened, fascinated as he pointed out all the horses.

"You really love it here, don't you?" she asked, eyeing him carefully, like she was actually seeing him, the real him, for the first time.

"I do." He stopped in front of his mare's stall and opened the door. "Meet Eleanor."

Eleanor pushed up against Mac. "Hey, girl," he said. "Have I not been giving you enough attention?" Eleanor whinnied and nudged Mac hard. He laughed and nearly fell backward. "She's got an attitude," he said to Jess.

She held her hand out. "Is it okay?"

"Sure." Mac patted his horse and Jess rubbed her nose and said, "She's beautiful. When is she due?"

"A couple of weeks."

"Hey, girl," she whispered to Eleanor, who seemed to take an instant liking to Jess. Not that he could blame her. Jess had such a calming, soothing demeanor. "Did you name her?" Jess asked.

He gave her a crooked grin. "Yeah, after my grandmother. She loved horses." His heart hitched when he caught the soft smile on her face. "What?" he asked.

"Nothing," she said as Eleanor kept nudging Mac. "Do you think we can take her for a walk?"

"Really?" he asked, liking that she cared so much about something that was important to him. "You want to?"

She nodded eagerly. "I'm a city girl and I never get the chance. Besides, I think she's trying to tell you something."

"I think you're right."

Mac strapped her up and they led her from the barn. He turned toward the mountain and guided Eleanor and Jess along a path until they were at the crest of a hill overlooking the ranch.

As Eleanor turned her attention to the grass, Jess stood near the edge taking in the view. She went quiet for a moment, introspective, then cast him a glance. "Why now, Mac?

After all these years, why did you arrange this, considering we haven't talked in ages?"

"We used to talk," he said. "Well, more like I talked, and you listened. But then things changed when we got older."

She pulled a face. "I guess you intimidated me."

"Why?"

"Because you became loud and wild."

He dropped to the ground and pulled her down with him. He stretched out, propping himself up on his elbows. "It was the only way to be heard most times." She gave him an odd look, and he went on to explain. "You were an only child. I grew up the youngest of six boys. If I wanted to be heard, I had to jump up and down and scream from the rooftops."

Understanding passed over her eyes. "I guess I never considered that. It was always so quiet at my place."

"I loved it at your place."

She smiled at nodded her head. "Because of the quiet, right?"

"Yeah, but that's not all."

"No?"

"No. I loved it because you were there."

"Oh," she said, her cheeks flushing again.

He gave her a sheepish look. "I always made an excuse to come over when Mom visited."

"She visited a lot to keep my mom company." She pursed her lips and added, "My father was away a lot."

When sadness entered her voice he asked, "Tell me about your dad. I never knew much about him."

"He was a salesman and a serious workaholic. I mean, my mom and I appreciated that he worked to take care of his family, but there should be a balance, know what I mean?"

When her eyes met his, he said, "I do. Could he have changed jobs, or at least positions in the company he worked for?"

"He did, and promised he'd be home more, but that never happened. Once a workaholic, always a workaholic."

"If I had a family at home, I'd learn to delegate more, because I'd always put them first."

She nodded, but he didn't get the sense that she believed him. She changed the subject and said, "For a guy who was always loud and boisterous, you seem pretty mellow right now."

He picked a blade of grass and put it between his teeth. "It's you, darlin'. You have this natural, soothing energy about you that relaxes people." He gestured with a nod toward his horse. "Just look at Eleanor. She's been so high-strung lately, and now she looks like she's about to nod off."

Jess laughed and cast a quick glance Eleanor's way. "She does look a bit tired." She looked back at the ranch below and went quiet.

"Tell me something," he asked, his smile falling.

She nibbled her lip, like she was worried about what he was going to ask. "What?"

He grabbed her hand and brushed his thumb over her flesh. Heat moved into her eyes, and he felt the shiver that moved through her. "Why did you really decide to stay?" he asked, so damn anxious to give her everything she'd ever wanted, needed, and get her to finally open up to him.

She blinked up at him, her eyes telling him what he needed to know. "Because I...I wanted to see...I needed to..."

"To explore the connection, too?" he asked.

"Yeah, something like that," she said.

When she nibbled her lip again and looked into the far distance to see Blake exiting the barn with the guests, he knew exactly what she was thinking. Even though he feared it might be a bit too soon, he said, "I have an idea."

She blinked up at him, and he could see intrigue in her eyes. "Should I be scared?"

"Never with me baby, never."

Chapter Four

Equal amounts of excitement and nervousness trickled through Jess's veins as she moved about her room getting ready for tonight's adventure. She had no idea what she would see, but she had to admit, she was anxious to find out more.

She knew that Wildman Mac would rock her world, and she had no doubt that, if she allowed herself to loosen up, she would experience more in one week with him than she had in her entire life. The truth was, everything about Mac intrigued her, from his contagious energy, the way he cared for his horse, to the way he leisurely gazed at her, desire brewing in the depths of his perceptive baby blues. God, no man had ever looked at her like that before, or had gone to such extreme measures to win her over. She had to admit, she was more than a little flattered by it all.

Of course, she couldn't forget that when the week was over, Mac would lose interest and move on, but she wasn't going to dwell on that, because it wasn't like she was here looking for long-term from him. No, Mac was a man who was on the road all the time, a workaholic like her father had been. She had seen the loneliness on her mother's face over the years, heard her tears even though she'd tried to hide her pain, and wanted no part of a life like that. Mac might have said he'd delegate more to put his family first, but honestly, she didn't think it was possible, not for someone with his personality. Truthfully, she and Mac were opposites in almost every way, and she'd be wise to remember that.

When Jess settled down, she wanted it to be with someone who put his family before his work, which meant that her plan and her only plan for this week was to abandon caution, try to push past her comfort zone, and let whatever was going to happen between them physically...*happen*. That last thought sent a shiver skittering through her.

Feeling restless, antsy, and completely on edge, she reapplied her lipstick and gave herself a once-over in the bathroom mirror. Since she wasn't sure what to wear to such a club, she opted for a simple black dress that touched the top of her knees, thankful that she'd decided to toss it into her suitcase at the last second.

She walked to her window to peer out and spotted Coop and Julia exiting the ranch's saloon. Julia had seemed quite nervous on the plane, but from the smile on her face now, to the intense way Coop was looking at her, Jess had no doubt he had one heck of an adventure waiting for her.

Just like Mac has one waiting for me.

Thinking of Mac had her remembering his peek into her journal—her innermost thoughts. She grabbed the leather-bound book off her bed and flipped it open, thumbing through the pages. She'd opened it to the middle when she handed it to him, and searched for the entry he might have read. Her breath caught when she scanned a few entries, and when she came across the one with the ménage, she gasped. Could he have read that? She dropped it onto her bed and paced back to her window. At the back of the lodge near the base of the mountain, she noticed a quaint cottage, but she had little time to consider who might live there when a hard knock sounded on her door.

She brushed her damp hands over her dress and tamped down her nervousness as she hurried across the room to answer. When she found Mac standing there staring at her, her breath caught in her throat, and a wave of nervousness rolled through her. She quickly pushed it away, and knowing she'd committed to this, wanted this, she was determined to follow through with their arrangement. With thumbs hooked in his front pockets, his stance was casual, relaxed, the look on his face completely flirtatious.

"Hey," he said, his smile making her weak in the knees. He leaned against the doorjamb and looked her over from head to toe.

"Hey yourself," she managed to get out. She crinkled her nose, suddenly uncomfortable as she took in his jeans and checkered shirt. "I think I'm overdressed."

He pushed off the door. "You look beautiful."

"Maybe I should change."

She made a move to go, but he stopped her. He slipped his hand around her waist and tugged her close. Her nipples pressed against his chest, and pressure brewed deep between her legs, a blatant reminder of how much she wanted to simply let go.

He dipped his head and whispered, "You don't have to change a thing, darlin'."

Overwhelmed by his close proximity and needing a moment of reprieve to gather herself, she croaked out, "Okay, just give me a second." When he released her, she darted to the bureau to grab her purse. She drew in a fortifying breath and turned back around, only to bump into a wall of muscle.

"Oh," she said, surprised to find Mac standing so close.

He captured her before she faltered, and as his big hand spread over her back, his glance momentarily flickered to the open journal on her bed. Her stomach soared, once again wondering which fantasies he'd read and if he really would fulfill them. With his expression unreadable, he looked back at her and fingered the silk material on the sleeve of her dress before trailing his hands down her arm. Her throat dried when she caught the intensity in his piercing eyes.

"Just so you know," he said, his voice heavy with desire, the air between them sexually charged, "I'll never make you do anything you're uncomfortable with."

She nodded, because beneath the heat in his eyes, there was real honesty. "Okay," she said.

Smile restored, he stepped back and waved a hand. "Then let's go."

He guided her to his truck, and after she climbed in, they drove away from the ranch. A few miles down the road, he turned to her and directed the conversation. "Did you know that your yoga studio is just around the corner from my office?"

She raised a challenging brow. "How is it you seem to know so much about me?"

He grinned. "I have my ways."

"Tell me about these ways."

"Jag's a private investigator."

"Ah, so that's how you three guys tracked us down after all these years."

"Yes and no." He shrugged, his look sheepish. "I've kind of been keeping tabs on you."

"Oh, really?" she said, a little surprised, and maybe a little pleased. But then again, she'd kept tabs on him, too.

She shot him an accusing glance. "What else do you know about me?"

He laughed. "Well, at the risk of sounding like a stalker, I know that you live alone and that early every morning, you go to the studio by yourself."

"So how come you never said hello?"

He arched a brow. "Do you really have to ask?"

Okay, okay, so they both knew she always ran in the opposite direction back in high school.

He gave her a wink, his look boyish and sweet when he admitted, "My charm never worked on you."

"And yet you invite me to your ranch for a whole week."

His grin was sly. "Yeah, because out here, no matter where you run, I can catch you."

She chuckled and glanced around the countryside as he drove. "Well, I must say I'm actually looking forward to tomorrow morning. I can imagine how peaceful it's going to be to meditate and go through my poses in the great outdoors with all the wildlife around me." She looked at the passing scenery and said, "Why don't you join me?"

He pulled a face. "Uh, because I'll probably end up twisted like a pretzel and rupture something I might need someday."

She laughed, loving the easy conversation between them. "Trust me. I teach the basics all the time. Besides," she added, touching his taut shoulder, "you're wound pretty tight, and yoga can help mellow you."

"Okay, but only if you promise not to make me do that downward dog pose I've heard about. Or the tree pose. I'd have to turn my man card in if I did something like that. But I'm game for whatever else you want to throw at me."

It surprised her that Mac wanted to join her in something important to her. It almost made her believe he was interested in her as a person, and there really was more to this reunion.

He went quiet for a moment and then laughed. "Speaking of mellow. Do you remember our old chemistry teacher, Mr. Sherry? The one who was always sucking on a cough drop?"

Jess made a snoring sound, then laughed along with him. "Could. He. Be. Anymore. Monotone."

"Bueller. Anyone? Anyone?" Mac added, grinning. "I'm not sure what he was making in that lab of his, but whatever it was it must have been some seriously good shit."

"I wonder what ever happened to him," Jess said.

"Last I heard he was working for a drug company. Getting rich off of making happy pills."

"Really?"

"Nah, I just made that up. Although it's probably true." Jess laughed, and Mac shook his head and added, "Actually, after a year with me in his class, he probably jumped from the highest bridge. That man did not like me."

"No wonder."

He feigned hurt. "Hey! What's that supposed to mean?"

She rolled her eyes. "Seriously, Mac. You must have

driven him crazy, always bouncing off the walls, messing with his Zen."

His blue eyes lit like a lightbulb had just gone off. "Maybe that's why he offered me a cough drop that day when I was being particularly obnoxious and screaming in the halls. My throat was hoarse but now I'm thinking those cough drops were his happy pills and he was trying to drug me."

"Did you have one?"

He gave her a look that suggested she was crazy for asking. "No, would you?"

"Of course. Cough drops made in a chemistry lab. What's not to love?"

As they both laughed, she sank further in her seat and stared at the road ahead. They continued to laugh and rehash old stories during the drive to the club, keeping things light as they talked about funny things that happened in their past.

Mac veered off the highway and drove another twenty miles down a long and winding road. Well on the outskirts of town, he pulled into a dark parking lot, squeezed his truck between two vehicles, and killed the engine. She glanced around and took in the lone brick building at the far end of the lot, WRANGLERS written on the small sign above the door.

He shifted in his seat, and his warm scent curled around her as he rested his hand on her backrest. Twirling a strand of her hair around his index finger, he asked, "You sure you want this?"

She clasped her hands tightly, guessing he picked up on her nervousness. "Yes," she said, not about to chicken out now.

"If at any time you want to leave, just let me know."

Her blood pulsed hot and a shiver moved through her, but it was a shiver from anticipation, not fear. "Okay."

"Just so you know, what happens at Wranglers stays at Wranglers."

"Oh," was all she could manage to say, curiosity and anticipation coursing through her.

When she nervously chewed on her bottom lip, his features softened. Caring blue eyes looked at her with genuine concern, and in a soft cadence he added, "Don't worry, Jess. Trust I'm going to take real good care of you."

A storm rolled through her as the promise in his voice touched her on another level. "I do," she said.

She reached for the door handle as Mac climbed from the cab and circled the front of the truck to meet her. He captured her hand in his, and they started toward the entrance. Music drifted from the open windows as they approached. Mac showed his ID at the door before signing Jess in to the members-only club. A moment later, he guided her through a set of double doors and into an upscale establishment that reminded her of a gentleman's club. Not that she'd ever stepped foot in one before, but she did watch a lot of old movies. Dark wood panels lined the walls and plush chairs were tucked into polished oak tables that were strategically positioned around a stage—a stage where half-naked women and men were dancing. To her left, there was a set of stairs leading to a loft. She glanced up and spotted numerous closed doors.

As she wondered what went on behind those closed doors, she glanced at the gorgeous cowgirls and cowboys sashaying across the stage, some performing acts on the brass poles.

"I didn't know there would be professional dancers."

He put his mouth close to her ear, and his warm breath washed over her face when he answered with, "They're not."

"No?"

"No. They're locals and they do it because some people like to be watched." He gestured with a nod to a crowd of both men and women seated close to the stage. "And some like to watch."

Her heart leaped as she thought about adding this naughty scenario to her journal. It was definitely one for her book, because in real life—even though she could relate to the desire to be watched—she was certain she would never have the courage to strip and perform for anyone.

As her eyes adjusted to the dim light, she noticed that the men and women were all in various stages of undress. She swallowed, the heavy scents of sex and cigars catching in her throat.

Mac squeezed her hand and shot her a reassuring glance, his eyes scanning her face like he knew her innermost thoughts. She felt a little nervous under his careful inspection.

They slipped into a booth at the back of the club, one that allowed them privacy while still giving them a great view of the stage. A waiter came by, and after asking what she'd like, Mac ordered drinks. He pulled her close, wrapping her in his heat as she scanned the club. Everything was so surreal she had a fear of awakening to find that none of it was real and she was back in her one-bedroom condo, immersed in one of her private fantasies.

"Everything okay?" Mac asked, his deep, sensual voice dragging her attention back to him.

"So this is how cowboys unwind," she murmured when

the waiter came back with a beer for Mac and a glass of wine for her.

"Cowgirls, too," he said, his glance falling over the pretty women on the stage.

At a table near the stage, Jess spotted a woman bent over her chair, her face a mask of pure ecstasy as her man moved over her from behind. She watched for a moment, and then understanding dawned.

"Wait, are they…?" she asked, hardly recognizing her voice.

The corner of his mouth twitched, hunger in his glance as he watched the couple with interest. "Yeah, baby. They are," he said. "Are you okay with that?"

The shock of what was happening lasted only a moment before lust settled in and consumed her. She squeezed her thighs together; the erotic action taking place in a room where all could watch was beyond anything she'd ever seen or written down. Unable to look away, Jess's fingers tightened on the edge of the table.

Mac touched her chin to draw her attention back to him. Something potent passed between them when he leaned close and whispered, "I take it you've never tried that."

She shot him a curious glance and thought about what it would be like for him to take her that way.

"Have you ever…" She reached for her wine, bringing it to her mouth with fingers that trembled. She cleared her throat. "Mac, do you come here often?"

"Not really." He grinned at her, and she leaned forward in the padded booth to take another quick sip of her drink, attempting to mimic Mac's casual pose as he stretched out beside her. "Are you nervous, darlin'?" he asked, his voice thick with desire.

"Yes," she answered.

"Do you want to leave?"

"No," she said quickly.

"Come here," he said, and pulled her to him.

Working to quell her nerves, she fell against him, his hand going to her thigh. As skin touched skin, her private parts came alive.

He pitched his voice low. "I'm guessing you've never been to a club like this."

She hesitated, finding it hard to keep a coherent thought with his hand so close to her sex. She shook her head no.

"But you wanted to, right?" Mac arched a knowing brow.

"What makes you say that?"

He slid his hand higher. His voice dipped to a sensual pitch. "The heat between your legs makes me say that, sweetheart. You're on fire."

D amned if he didn't want to give her a night to remember. The first of many, he hoped.

As her eyes dimmed with need, he wondered just how far she'd like to go tonight. He knew that deep down, she wanted to be a part of all this, and while he'd asked for her submission, he wasn't about to push too hard and frighten her off.

"Do you see something you like?" he asked as she zeroed in on Blake and two pretty blond girls who were staying at the ranch. The three were all wrapped up in one another on the dance floor, their bodies simulating sex as they moved and gyrated to the music.

Her throat worked as she swallowed, and her chest heaved as she watched the action.

"Jess?"

"Yeah?" she asked, like she was having a hard time focusing on conversation as people around them became intimate.

"Do you see something you like?" he asked again, and that's when Blake turned their way and caught her staring. His friend whispered something to the girls, and then made his way over to their table.

He cast Mac a knowing grin. "I thought you said you weren't coming?"

"Change of plans," Mac said, scrubbing his jaw.

Blake turned to Jess, his smile slow and inviting. "The lady looks like she wants to dance." He shot Mac a quick look as he held his hand out to Jess. "You don't mind, do you?"

Fuck yeah, he minded. He minded a lot. He glared at Blake. Sure, they'd done this kind of thing before, and he'd never been a possessive man, until now…until Jess. But how could he say no? Jess had been watching him intently, with interest, and he wanted to give her what she wanted.

Before Mac could answer, Blake grabbed her hand and gave a tug.

"Oh, okay," Jess said, and when she slid from the booth, she fell against Blake. He gave Mac a grin as he led her to the dance floor, and Mac clenched his jaw as he watched his pal lead his girl away. Blake pulled her in closer, and Mac sucked in a sharp breath as he worked to get his shit together. Christ, there was no way Blake could know how much it bothered him to see Jess in his arms, considering all the times they'd tag-teamed in the past.

The music changed, became slower, and Blake splayed his hands over her back, coming perilously close to her sweet ass. Oh hell no! That sweet ass was *his*. Mac climbed from his seat and moved through the throng to come up to her from behind. As he pressed his chest into her back, he felt a tremble move through her, a tremble that told him so goddamn much. Fuck, she liked this. She liked being between the two of them. Not that it really surprised him. Not after reading her journal. There was no doubt he wanted Jess for himself, but if he wanted to show her he cared, then he'd do whatever he had to, to give her what *she* wanted.

"Hey," Mac said, whispering into her ear.

He gripped her hips and spun her around to face him, and when he caught the flush on her cheeks, the two girls Blake had been dancing with earlier came back to hijack him.

Blake laughed, and before they dragged him off he said, "I'll catch up with you for a beer later."

Mac pulled her in tight, and as her body pressed against him, his cock swelled. She sucked in a breath and turned when a couple beside them moaned. He felt her shudder as the half-naked duo began to rock against each other. As the man's hand moved beneath the woman's skirt, a small sound caught in Jess's throat.

"Do you like what you see?" Mac asked.

She turned back to Mac and when he saw the way her eyes dimmed with desire, he widened her legs with his knee, sensing she wanted the same. She moved against his leg, desire dancing in her eyes. His mouth found hers and he kissed her deeply. As their tongues tangled, he explored her body, running his hands along her curves. He lifted her hands and put them above her head, then ran his fingers down the length of them, dragging his thumbs over the outer swell of her breasts.

He felt her stiffen, and inched back to see her.

She blinked, and as her breathing grew rapid, she stole another glance around the club. Her smile fell. "I...uh...I have to go."

He clenched his jaw hard enough to grind bone, his bliss disappearing as he tucked a strand of hair behind her ear, wanting to assure her everything was okay.

"Which way is the bathroom?" she asked as she inched away from him.

Without giving him time to answer, she darted toward the hall.

Fuck.

He was about to go after her when Blake came back. "Who the hell is she, and where did she come from?"

He watched her disappear around the corner, and when she was out of his sight he sent his friend a quick glance. "I grew up with her."

Blake shook his head, his eyes full of disbelief. "You've known her for years, and I'm just now getting to meet her?"

"I've been crazy about her my entire life," Mac admitted. She'd been the first girl he'd fantasized about, fallen for. And even though he hadn't talked to her in years, he'd always thought about her. Kept tabs on her to make sure she was okay. Now that he'd had a taste, he only craved more.

Blake nodded. "Yeah, I can see why. And I guess I can see why you've been keeping her to yourself. But I think your girl wants to play."

"We'll play," Mac said, looking back down the hall where Jess had disappeared, and hoping like hell he hadn't blown things between them. He turned to Blake, looking him dead in the eyes. "But you should know…this time, I'm playing for keeps."

Blake's head came back with a start. "You're fucking kidding me."

Mac gave a slow shake of his head. "Nope, not even a little."

"So she's hands-off then?"

"Yes, and no," Mac said, and leaned toward his friend, wanting only to do right by Jess and give her what she really wanted.

A few minutes later, after explaining his plan to Blake, Mac went to collect her. "I'll catch up with you later," he said, then made his way toward the bathroom.

When she came out and found him standing there, a gasp caught in her throat.

"Jess," he said, everything inside him reaching out to her when she blinked up at him with bright-eyed innocence. "I'm sorry." He shook his head and pulled her against him. "I thought you were ready for this. You seemed curious, so I thought—"

"Mac," she whispered.

"Yeah, baby," he murmured.

"I want to go."

"I know," he said, putting his arm around her waist to lead her toward the door.

She stopped in her tracks. "No, Mac," she said, her lashes dipping lower over her dark bedroom eyes. "I want to go…" She paused, took a deep breath, and nodded toward the loft upstairs. "Up there."

When she parted her lips in a silent invitation, conveying without words what she wanted, his heart thudded in his chest. Thrilled, yet hardly able to believe this turn of events, his mouth crashed down on hers, not about to waste another second. He kissed her long and hard, pushing his knee between her legs.

She rocked against his knee, her movements sexy and intimate as he continued to kiss her. Her breasts scraped over his chest, and he pulled back, drew a shaky breath, and said, "Let's go."

Walking quickly, he guided her down the hall and up the winding staircase until he reached his private room. He pulled his key card from his pocket and noticed the look on her face.

"Change of heart?" he asked.

"No," she said, her tone soft. "I'm just wondering why you have a key when you said you don't come here often."

"Every member gets one, but this is my first time using it."

"Oh, I didn't mean…it doesn't matter…I was just…"

"Jess," he said to stop her, placing one hand on her cheek, eager to gain all her trust. "I would never lie to you." Her body relaxed slightly, and he turned his attention to the lock. He swiped the card and when the light turned green, he pushed the door open and ushered her into the room. He set the lock and turned to look at her. Gone was that brief moment of hesitation, and in its place existed need. His hands went to his shirt as his eyes latched onto her sexy curves.

"I want you naked. Now."

Chapter Five

Pressed against the door in a dimly lit room with nothing more than a king-size bed smack-dab in the center of it, Jess watched Mac undress. Honestly, she couldn't quite believe that she was here with him, but there was no denying that she wanted this.

With that last thought in mind, she pushed off the door and shed her dress, but her hands stilled on her bra strap when he removed his pants to expose the biggest cock she'd ever set eyes on. It was true that she hadn't been with many men, but those she had climbed between the sheets with failed to compare to the Adonis standing before her.

"Come here," he said, his voice a little rough.

"Mac," she croaked as she crossed the room to meet him. Deft hands quickly unhooked her bra, and he cupped her breasts.

He paused and met her glance. "Are you sure, sweetheart? I want you so much that once I start it's going to be hell to stop."

"I'm sure," she whispered.

A low growl sounded in his throat as he bent down and pulled one hard nipple into his mouth. Her hands went to his hair, and she grabbed a fistful of his dark strands as he hungrily teased her nipples, his hands sliding down her sides to shape her contours.

He sucked harder, and she arched into him. "So good," she cried out, desperate to feel his impressive girth inside.

Her hands slid to his shoulders, and she palmed his muscles. She gasped as he ripped her panties from her hips and tossed them away. His hands moved hungrily over her body and halted at the juncture between her legs.

When she widened for him, he groaned. She rubbed herself against his hand, desperate for more.

"Tell me what you want," he said, as he sank to his knees to press heated kisses to her stomach. "Tell me exactly what you want, and I'll give it to you, darlin'."

She'd never had the nerve to vocalize the naughty things she'd written in her journal. A sudden bout of shyness overcame her.

"Tell me now," he growled. His kisses pushed away the last of her reserve.

Jess swallowed. He was offering her a once-in-a-lifetime fantasy, was willing to give her everything she'd ever wanted if she'd only ask. She pulled in a fortifying breath and forced herself to blurt out, "I want your mouth on my pussy."

He sucked in a sharp breath and stilled for a moment. Quiet hovered over them, and she sensed he was fighting for a measure of control when he demanded, "Say it again."

"I want your—"

"No," he said. "Say pussy."

Her heart leaped, excited by his heated reaction. She watched a tremor move through his body and realized how much she wanted this.

"Pussy," she murmured. "I want you to lick my pussy."

There was a sense of urgency about him when he climbed to his feet and gathered her into his arms. He took three long strides, and then gently tossed her on the bed.

God, she loved the way he was going all primal on her, taking full control of their play. As her own basic elemental needs took hold, she went up on her elbows to watch him climb between her legs.

"Open for me, baby," he murmured, then buried his face between her thighs. His mouth felt like fire on her skin as he pressed a kiss over her sex.

"Oh, God," she cried out, her hips coming off the mattress.

His thumb circled her clit, his tongue swirling over her in the most tantalizing ways—ways no man had ever done before. Unable to think with any sort of clarity as he indulged in her body, she gripped the bedding beneath her, her breath coming in quick little pants.

"Christ, you have no idea how long I've wanted to taste you," he murmured from between her legs. He cast her a hot glance, and there was something very erotic in the way he licked his lips. "Sweet," he murmured. "So fucking sweet."

Taking pleasure in watching him feast on her, her hands crushed his hair, holding him between her legs. Feeling crazed, frantic, she placed one of her hands on her breast and squeezed her nipple, sending tingles all the way down her body. He continued to do delicious things with his tongue, and as he unleashed the vixen in her, she writhed, seeking something else.

"I need you inside me," she blurted out without censor, impatience thrumming through her. "Please, Mac, I...I... need you to fuck me."

Her hands raced over his shoulders, and his entire body trembled, his muscles bunching. "Jesus," he cursed from between her legs. "You can't say that to me."

"Why not?"

"Because I'll lose it, that's why."

It thrilled her to see Mac losing it, that she was the one doing it to him. "Please, Mac. Please fuck me..."

Without speaking, he climbed from the bed to grab his pants off the floor. He took out a condom, and after sheathing himself, he slid up her body and pressed down on her, holding her captive beneath him. With his cock positioned at her opening, his eyes met hers, and something very intimate passed between them, something that had her heart racing and her brain warning her that it might not be so easy to walk away when this week was over. She took a sharp breath and reminded herself that Mac was incapable of more than a quick, hot affair.

The muscles along his jaw twitched, and she turned her focus to the desire burning through her when his mouth met hers. Entirely lost in the moment, she lifted her hips, and he growled as his tip breached her opening.

He gave her an inch. "Is this what you want, sweetheart?"

"More," she cried out, bucking against him, and with that, he plunged deep, driving into her so hard and fast it drove the breath from her lungs.

His kisses were hard and demanding. He pumped into

her, and she lifted her hips, meeting each powerful thrust. His cock brushed over the bundle of nerves inside her, and she couldn't believe how gloriously full she felt. Mac grabbed a fistful of her hair and continued to pound hard, like he couldn't get deep enough.

Sensations ripped through her, and she hardly recognized her own voice when she whimpered, "So good."

He slipped a hand between them, and the pleasure was exquisite when he found her clit. He rammed into her, reaching a fevered pitch until she was crying out his name. She quivered beneath his ministrations, the length of his shaft stroking deeper than any before him, and when he applied extra pressure to her swollen nub, the rippling waves of an orgasm took hold. Her erotic whimper filled the room; a second later, she clenched hard around his cock. Her mind soared. Everything but this man and what he was doing to her faded from existence.

"Fuck," he ground out, and she could tell he was working hard to keep it together. But she wanted him to come unglued, wanted him to feel as crazed as her.

She wrapped her legs around him and held him tight as she rode out the waves, taking her higher and higher. When he closed his eyes, she thrust her pelvis forward, forcing him in deeper, and whispered, "I want to feel you come inside me."

His low growl curled around her, and his corded muscles bunched as he buried his face in her neck. She could feel the rapid-fire pounding of his heart against her chest as he climaxed high inside her, and it didn't go unnoticed that sex between them felt more intimate than anything she'd ever known. She ran her hands over his back, reveling in his every spasm as he depleted himself.

He dropped down on top of her. He captured her mouth in a slow, simmering kiss before leisurely rolling off. When he turned to her, emotions gathered in a knot in her stomach. She swallowed, loving the way he looked at her, wanted her.

"Jess," he whispered, a warm palm cupping her cheek. "I knew it would be good, baby. But it was even better than good."

"Yeah, I know," she murmured, contentment coursing through her veins as she snuggled closer.

"I never lost it so fast before," he said.

She reached out and touched him, marching her fingers over his chest. He was such a giving lover, putting her needs first and taking her to places she'd only ever dreamed about.

Sexy and rumpled, with a grin that made him look boyish, he touched her hair, pushing it from her face. "I love the way you opened up tonight."

"You're a man of many talents," she said, giving a lazy, catlike stretch. But she couldn't get too comfortable. She had to remind herself this was temporary. While they were good—great—together in the bedroom, it certainly didn't mean they'd make great life partners. Even if he was serious about wanting more, which she still doubted, there was a lot more to relationships than good sex, and she wanted a man who would put his family first.

"Come on," he said, slipping off the side of the bed.

"Where we going?" she asked.

"Back to the ranch. I have to check on Eleanor." He gave her a grin full of mischief and promise. "Then there are so many more things I'm going to do with you."

After returning to the ranch, Mac walked Jess to her room so she could get changed and he made her promise to meet him at the saloon later. He stood outside her bedroom door long after she'd closed it, and listened to her move around inside as his mind went over everything that had just happened. He took a deep breath and let it out slowly. Totally blown away by Jess and the things they did at Wranglers. Jesus, he knew sex between them would be good, but it was even better than he expected. So much better, in fact, it scared him a little, even though he wanted more from her. He ran a shaky hand through his hair and forced himself to push away from her door and make his way outside to the barn.

Twenty minutes later, after checking on his mare, Mac left the barn in time to see Jess exit the lodge and head toward the saloon. Loud country music spilled from the open windows, and as she approached the door, he hurried his steps to get there first.

He felt a shudder move through her body when he put his mouth close to her ear and whispered, "Allow me, ma'am."

He pulled the door open and settled his hand on the small of her back as he led her inside. When she saw a stage set up near the bar, she turned to Mac. "What's going on?"

"Karaoke night," he explained.

She shook her head. "I'm not going up there."

Ignoring her protest, he said, "Come on, let's have a drink."

He guided her to a table in the corner, and when Tamara the waitress came by, Mac put their order in. Jess grinned as she listened to one of the guests massacre a song, and when the crowd broke out in laughter, his heart tightened, loving the way her smile lit up her pretty face.

After their drinks arrived, he shifted closer. His worries that things were moving too fast for her—hell, for him— disappeared as she leaned into him. He pulled her in tight, reveling in the new comfort between them. They watched guest after guest take the stage, and after she finished her drink, he knew it was their turn. He climbed to his feet and dragged her with him.

"No way," she said.

He put his mouth close to her ear. "My rules, my way," he reminded her. Then he softened his voice and added, "And don't worry, I'm coming with you."

Her dark eyes met his, and he smiled at her, encouraging her to break out of her shell and try something new. They exchanged a long, thoughtful look.

She drew a breath and let it out slowly. "Okay," she said with a hint of nervousness edging her voice.

He took her to the stage, and she hung back a bit as he looked through the music. Once he found a song from their high school days, he grabbed a microphone for himself and handed her one.

Mac started singing first, so out of tune the crowd started booing him. He turned to find Jess grinning, and he shot her a pleading look. "I need help here," he said.

She shook her head at him, put the microphone to her lips, and began singing along quietly. When the patrons heard her voice, they all began clapping. She grinned, and her voice grew a little stronger. Mac slipped his arm around her waist, holding her to him as they belted out the lyrics.

Halfway through the song, Jess messed up the words, and shot him an embarrassed look. Mac waved his hands toward the crowd, gesturing for them to shout encouraging words. They clapped, and even though heat stained her cheeks, she smiled with them, and then quickly picked up where she left off.

He listened to her sing, her beautiful angel voice so pleasing to the patrons. He felt a tightness in his chest, right around the vicinity of his heart. Of course, he'd known all along that she could carry a tune, having caught her singing in the music room after all the other students had left. She was normally shy and hated putting herself in the spotlight, which was why he'd brought her here tonight. She'd opened herself up to him in the bedroom, and now he wanted her to open herself up outside of it.

When the song ended, she was ready to pass the microphone off to the two women waiting their turn—the two petite Barbie-doll blondes who'd been with Blake earlier—but the crowd clapped, demanding more. Jess blinked up at him, her nose crinkling in the cutest way. "What do I do?"

"How about one more?" he whispered. "They love you." Damned if he could blame them.

"Okay," she agreed, and he was certain he saw pleasure backlighting her eyes.

He picked another song.

As they belted out the lyrics once again, he noticed the small sway to her hip. As he watched her open up, actually enjoy herself, his heart swelled with pride.

When they finished and the two women took to the

stage, they both handed off their microphones. Mac pulled her in close and asked, "Want to get out of here?"

She nodded, and he led her outside.

He nudged her and said, "You did good."

She smiled at him and teased, "I wish I could say the same for you."

He laughed and whacked her ass. "Hey!"

After she laughed, she went quiet and said, "Actually, I can't believe I did that, but it was kind of fun."

"You should let loose more often."

"Maybe I will." she said.

The chorus of birds pulled Jess from her slumber. She opened her eyes and blinked against the early-morning light spilling in through the slit in the curtains. Shifting on the comfy mattress, she stretched out her limbs, and when her hand connected with hard, warm flesh, every delicious memory from last night came rushing back, and not just sexual ones. Her body ached in the most intimate places, but it was the pounding of her heart that really caught her attention.

She rolled onto her side and couldn't help but smile as she perused him. Flat out on his back with his arms above his head, he slept quietly. While she wanted to wake him, to touch his hard body all over again and feel him inside her, she couldn't bring herself to do it. Not when he looked so relaxed and peaceful. Besides, after all the things they'd done together last night, from the club, to the singing, he deserved a little rest.

She slipped from the bed and without bothering to dress, quietly walked to the window. Off in the distance, she spotted someone swimming in the lake and wondered who else would be up at such an early time of morning. Padding softly to the bathroom, she brushed her teeth and washed up, anxious to get outside and do her morning stretches before the other guests surfaced.

Moving to her suitcase, she rooted through her belongings and caught the corner of her journal peeking out from beneath her clothes, having hidden it in there last night when she and Mac returned from the club. Normally, she'd spend the night tucked under her covers writing out a forbidden fantasy, but last night, she'd indulged in one instead.

She dressed quickly and grabbed her yoga gear. Mac shifted on the mattress. As she stared at him, taking in the stubble shadowing his jaw, she couldn't help but grin and notice how close she felt to him, their open lovemaking and the way they both laid themselves bare taking them to a whole new level of intimacy, one she'd never experienced before. Everything in what they did left her feeling sexy and adventurous, but it also left her yearning for so much more.

She sucked in a breath to pull herself together. Hadn't she lectured herself on enjoying this for what it was—sex—and keeping her emotions out of it? With that last thought in mind, she tiptoed from the room and made her way outdoors. Breathing in the fresh air, she walked past the horse stable. Inside, she heard a rustling sound and wondered if it was Blake moving about and getting ready for his day.

She thought back to last night, to the way Mac had sandwiched her between him and Blake. A fine shiver moved through her as she considered being with two men, both of them touching her, pleasuring her, putting their mouths all over her body. She tightened. Good God, she could hardly believe how much that excited her. But even after all she'd done with Mac, she'd never have the courage to share that seductive fantasy with him.

She made her way toward the eastern mountain. After finding the path Mac had taken her and Eleanor up, she climbed to the top. She dropped her towel, put her earbuds in, and turned on her iPod. She tipped her face to the sun and took a moment to concentrate on her breathing. She lifted her arms above her head, stretching out her well-used muscles. Shelving all her work worries and concentrating only on the slow, relaxing music, she let the sounds soothe her soul.

Halfway into her routine, completely lost in the moment, a strong male arm slipped around her body from behind, pinning her arms to her sides as he pulled her against his chest. She froze for a second and then let loose a strangled cry.

"Hey, baby, it's just me," Mac whispered, pulling one of her earbuds out and dangling it in front of her face. "I called out but you didn't hear me."

She whipped around to face him and yanked the earpiece from his fingers. "You scared the life out of me."

He gave her a sheepish look. "Sorry."

"How did you know where to find me?"

"I guessed." He held up a backpack. "I brought breakfast. Does that get me off the hook for scaring you?"

She drew a breath to gather herself. "I suppose. But first, I need to finish my routine."

He put the backpack down and rubbed his hands together. "Let's do it, then."

She arched a brow. "You're going to do it with me?"

"I told you last night I wanted to, but you didn't wake me."

"I thought you needed your sleep."

He gave her a wink and teased. "Oh, now I see. You let me sleep so I'd be good and rested for tonight?"

She laughed and cocked her head. "Are you sure you're up for this?"

"Yeah, as long as you take it easy on me." When she folded her arms in challenge, he said, "We'll save the hard stuff for later."

"Be good or I'll make you do downward dog pose."

"As long as we can do it my way," he murmured playfully, but clamped his mouth shut when she cast him a warning glance.

She proceeded to show him a few basic moves, and she had to admit, as he practiced his breathing exercises, she could almost feel the tension drain from him, filling his type-A personality with a new kind of calm.

She spoke in soft tones, drawing him into her peaceful, tranquil state. She continued with the poses, and he mimicked them, although he didn't quite have her flexibility or stretch. Regardless, she was sure he'd never been more relaxed in his life.

She taught him to clear his mind as the sun warmed their muscles, and they listened to the animals and the soft whisper of the wind drifting by on a breeze.

By the time they finished the routine, his stomach started grumbling, and Jess laughed. "I think we'd better feed you."

"I think that's a good idea." He found a nice, flat grassy spot near the edge of the cliff overlooking the ranch. As Jess looked out over the view, her body so warm and relaxed, Mac opened his backpack to pull out fruit, a thermos full of coffee, and bagels and blueberry cream cheese.

"Do you come to the ranch often?" she asked.

"As much as I can."

"What made you all buy a working dude ranch in the middle of nowhere?"

"Coop's mom isn't well. We all went splits on the ranch because this is where Coop thought she'd be most comfortable since she grew up in farm country.

Surprised that he'd go to such extremes for a friend, warmth and respect moved through her. "I had no idea." She went quiet for a moment, thinking more about the boy from her youth. "You're a good friend."

And an amazing man…

Mac shrugged the compliment away and spread some cheese over a sliced bagel. "It was a sound investment," he said, handing Jess the bread. "Come on, let's eat, I'm starving."

"Thanks." Jess took the morning treat and bit into it, savoring the explosion of flavors on her tongue. She didn't comment on the gruffness in his voice or the flush on his cheeks. He was a man who did things for others out of kindness and uncomfortable with compliments. To lighten the mood, she bumped shoulders with him and took another bite. "You can really build up an appetite doing yoga."

"Yeah, well, I was hungry before we started. Watching you did that to me."

She arched a brow. "Oh? And just how long were you watching me?"

His grin was wolfish. "Long enough to make me

ravenous."

The gleam in his eyes told her he wasn't talking about food.

She grabbed the Styrofoam cups and divided up the coffee. When he rolled one shoulder she asked, "How do you feel?"

"Pretty damn good, actually." He looked over his body. "And I don't think I ruptured anything. You're a great teacher. Your students must love you."

At the mention of her work, and the possibility of losing her business because she had no idea how to market herself or the skills to bring in new clients, her stomach clenched.

"What?" he asked.

She immediately wiped away the sadness, not wanting to spoil the calmness of the moment. "Nothing."

As she sipped her coffee, he spread cream cheese onto another bagel and handed it to her.

"Mmm," she said and took a generous bite. "These are so good." He placed his hand on her leg and gave it a squeeze. Feeling completely comfortable with him, she said, "I'm glad you joined me."

He leaned back on one elbow and said, "So am I."

"And last night...the club...well..." she began, as she toyed with her cup.

"What about it?"

"I'm glad you took me." She bit the corner of her lip. "Was that...what you read...in my journal?"

"Maybe, or maybe I just know a lot more than you realize." He took a huge bite of his bagel and washed it down with a swig of coffee.

She chewed and then nodded slowly. "I'm beginning to

believe that."

"You have an adventurous spirit, Jess. I've always known that about you."

"How?"

He smiled. "I have a confession to make."

"You do?"

"Last night at the club, it wasn't just your reactions to what was going on around you or the heat between your legs that told me what you wanted."

"No?"

"No. Years ago, I kind of sneaked a peek over your shoulder and glimpsed what you were writing in your journal." He touched her face, running the rough pad of his thumb over her cheek. "Plus I saw the kinds of books you were reading when you weren't writing."

She could feel color move into her cheeks. "You...you did?"

"Yeah, and I went to an out-of-town bookstore to grab a copy."

Her eyes widened. "So you knew?"

"Yeah, I knew." He nudged her and said, "And I liked it, Jess. Jesus, here it is years later and my fingers are still scorched from turning the pages."

She nibbled her lip. "I can't believe you went through so much trouble."

"Well, I couldn't buy them at home. The guys would have taken my man card and sacked me on the football field."

She laughed. "From what I saw, they sacked you a lot as it was."

He laughed with her. "Football wasn't really my thing, but I liked being on the team." He stopped laughing and said "Wait, you were watching me?"

"Maybe…"

All humor gone from his tone, he said, "I used to look for you after practice, to give you a ride home, but when I found you…well, I didn't want to disturb you."

She furrowed her brow, her mind racing a million miles an hour. "You were in the school after hours?"

"Yeah."

When understanding dawned, she said, "That's how you knew about my singing."

"That's right," he confessed. "I loved listening to you."

"I can't believe you heard me singing…peeked at my journal."

"About your journal, Jess. Tell me, is there anything specific in it that you'd like to share with me, that you'd like me to do?"

Her chest rose and fell erratically as she scanned the ranch, her glance settling on Blake as he exited the barn.

Mac followed her gaze. "If you liked the club, we can go again," he said. "Maybe there are some other things you'd like to try there."

For a brief second she thought she spotted tension in his jaw; then he ran his hand over his face, and it was gone.

A noise in the valley below drew her attention. The two women who took over the karaoke machine after Jess last night, the same women from the club, met Blake near the corral. As they ran their hands over him, making no qualms about what they wanted, he slid his arms around their waists and led them inside one of the barns.

Jess grinned. "I take it Blake is the jack-of-all-trades around here?"

"You could say that."

"Where to now?"

"First, I have to check on Eleanor, then we have some chores to do."

"We?"

"This is a working dude ranch, you know. Did you think you were getting off easy?"

"Well, so far I've been getting off pretty easy," she teased.

When he laughed, she flushed, unable to believe that she'd say something so bold, so sexy, but there was just something about Mac that made it so easy to relax around him and let go of her inhibitions.

Chapter Six

After spending the day helping Mac with chores around the ranch and falling into bed for another round of lovemaking, Jess awoke feeling gloriously content. She stretched her body out, and even though Mac had insisted he join her in her early-morning stretches, she was certain his muscles really did need the rest.

She climbed from her bed, pulled on her gear, and left her room. She walked along the large expanse of ranch, taking in the beauty, and this morning, instead of climbing the mountain, she decided to do her routine in a secluded spot tucked beneath the crest overlooking the ranch. Once there, she turned her music on and began her routine. Less than twenty minutes later, she felt a body move against hers. At first she assumed it was Mac, until a blindfold was placed over her eyes.

Her breath caught and she tensed. Her earbuds were removed and a voice whispered, "Shh." She turned her face toward him and pulled a breath in through her nose. The familiar fragrance of citrus and soap assailed her senses. *Mac.* Desire replaced the alarm. Ribbons of heat moved down her spine.

She sucked in an excited breath, but she felt another person step in front of her, blocking the warm sun from her body, and she suddenly found herself sandwiched between two walls of muscle. She gasped, sucking in air as she realized the scenario was right out of her private journal.

Was this what he'd read?

"What are you doing?" she asked breathlessly, almost too excited to speak when he began to walk her backward.

"You have nothing to worry about, baby. I'm going to take good care of you. I promise you that," Mac said. A moment later, he slipped out from behind her, and she felt herself being pressed against the towering mountain, the heat from the warm rock wall seeping under her skin, arousing her all the more. With her vision blocked, her other senses became finely tuned. She felt something rough brush over her arms before her wrists were bound and secured over her head.

She tugged at the rope, discovered that she could, if she chose to, pull her hands free, but the thought of being restrained by two cowboys had pleasure zinging through her. "What—"

"Easy there," the other man said. She recognized Blake's voice.

Oh. My. God. Her pulse leaped in her throat, hardly able to believe what was happening. This had to be what he'd read, and the fact that he was playing it out for her, going so far as to solicit the help of another man, touched her in ways that left her feeling a little shaky, a little emotional.

"Mac," she whispered past the lump in her throat as her heart swelled. God, there was so much more to this man than she knew. He was sweet, funny, kind, and so giving. He was everything a girl could ever want.

"Now you be a real good girl, and do as I say," Mac whispered, his voice loaded with promise. A hand stroked her breasts, and she knew from the way Mac touched her before that it wasn't his hand on her body. Through her shirt, Blake lightly surfed his finger over her nipple until she found herself arching into him, giving herself over to the pleasure he was offering.

"Easy, sweetheart," Blake said, his mouth close to her ear, his warm, familiar scent feeding the hunger inside her. "No need to rush things. We've got all day to play."

Warm lips found hers. Blueberries and cream cheese. *Mac.* She moved her hips and returned the kiss, thinking how easily she could lose herself in him.

Moisture pooled between her thighs, and she squirmed, seeking relief for the ache building there. The restraint securing her arms rubbed against her skin, and while she loved being held captive by these two men, she wanted to touch them, to feel their rippled muscles beneath her fingers.

"Do you like that, baby?" Mac asked, slipping a hand between her legs. "Do you like having us both touch you?"

"Yes." She whimpered and wiggled against the wall to prove how much she liked it.

"Good. I'm going to keep the blindfold on for now because I want you to just feel and enjoy," he said, a tenderness in his tone she'd never heard before. He pressed a soft, loving kiss to her mouth, a kiss so gentle and affectionate it took her breath away.

Before raw emotions could get the better of her, someone lifted her shirt. She sucked in a breath as a breeze washed over her bare skin, tightening her already-hard nipples. Mac's and Blake's groans of pleasure merged, exciting her all the more.

"Beautiful," Blake said, and a moment later, she felt his hot, wet mouth on her breast. Then, when she felt Mac's lips close around her other nipple, the dual assault nearly drove her over the edge.

"Oh my God," she murmured, working to keep a modicum of composure as her entire world flipped upside down. Scorching mouths laved her buds, and a need so powerful it was almost frightening gathered in her stomach. She closed her eyes against the flood of emotions and concentrated on the pleasure…*so much pleasure.*

Mac's mouth left her body, and she immediately missed his warmth on her nipple, but Blake's hand closed over her bare breast, kneading it with deep hunger. Mac's thick fingers dipped inside the band of her pants, pushing them downward, and she whimpered with need. He dragged them lower, and when he reached her ankles he said, "Lift your leg, sweetheart." She immediately obliged. He removed her pants and slid her panties down, nudging her clit in the process. A moment later, she stood before the two, completely bare in so many ways.

Mac pressed his mouth to her ear again, and she shivered as his hands moved over her body as though reacquainting himself with her curves. His fingers burned everywhere he touched. She wet her lips, need careening through her.

"Widen your legs for me. Show me how much you want

it."

A breeze curled around her thighs, cooling the hot moisture between her legs when she opened them. Mac's lips captured hers, his kiss deep and sensual as Blake pushed against her side. Her heart stuttered when she felt his thick cock press into her hip. Ecstasy flitted through her. She was trapped in a web of sensation, enslaved by two aroused cowboys eager to please her and give her the ultimate fantasy.

She breathed in the scents of the men, the combination of citrus and soap and spice and musk driving her wild. When a set of teeth clamped around her nipple, she gasped, her back arching against the wall. Soft licks followed, soothing the sting, and she was sure she'd never felt anything quite so sensuous.

Her skin flushed. A hand moved across her hip, down the crease of her thigh, and slid between her legs, feathering the moistened curls at the very edge of her sex. Jess wiggled her hips, seeking a firmer caress. The hand retreated.

"What do you want?" The soft query tickled her ear.

Mac.

"Please." Blistering heat careened through her blood with a force that left her feeling light-headed.

"Please, what?" His hand dipped, skimmed the curls, and retreated again.

She rocked her hips, frustration warring with desire. "Please, touch me."

"Where, Jess? Where do you want to be touched?"

"My…"

"Say it," he demanded in a soft voice.

Not wanting to be that reserved girl here with Mac, she drew a breath and said, "I need you to touch my pussy. I need you to put your fingers inside me."

She listened to Mac's throat work as he swallowed. "You're a very bad girl, aren't you?" he asked, the lust in his tone curling her toes.

"Yes, I—" she began, but her voice fell off when the rough pad of his finger slicked over her hot clit.

Another hand joined his between her legs, and she widened more to accommodate both men. A thick finger pushed inside, and she rested her head against the rock wall, not caring which cowboy was burrowing deep—only that they were finally answering the demands of her body.

Her blindfold was removed, and she caught Mac's glance. His jaw was clenched, and he had a look she couldn't quite identify on his face when he asked, "Do you want to watch?"

She nodded and glanced down to see his finger join Blake's inside her. She cried out loud as the two began to move in sync, pushing high inside her and pleasuring her in the most erotic ways.

Blake's hand slipped around her body, but Mac stopped him. "Only me," he said in a hoarse voice that caught Jess's attention. "And her mouth, that's mine, too." Blake nodded, and withdrew his hand. Mac caressed her ass, and her mouth fell open when he lightly stroked her puckered passage. He toyed with her, letting her get used to the feel before he inched a finger inside her. She cast questioning eyes his way, wondering if he was going to enter her from behind.

Not that she'd say no. She wanted to do this, to experience everything with Mac while she could.

His mouth found her neck, and he pushed his cock against her hip as he played with her pussy and ass simultaneously.

God, everything in the way these men indulged in her body, touching her all over, not daring to miss a speck of flesh, made her feel so sensuous, so special, so eager to do anything...*everything*. A maelstrom of sensation overcame her as Blake dropped to his knees to take her clit into his mouth.

He bit down on her engorged nub, and her skin tightened beneath his invading mouth. She threw her head back and pitched her hips forward. Mac slipped his finger deeper inside her back passage. A moan caught in her throat. Oh, God, she'd never felt so full before, both men dipping into her body in such a delicious manner. Uninhibited, and wanting to be ravished at the base of this mountain with the wildlife scurrying around her, she moved her hips as they indulged in her flesh, the sweet torture pushing her to the precipice in record time.

Mac's cock throbbed against her hip, and passion and possessiveness gleamed in his eyes. "You like that, baby?"

"Yes," she cried out, and his lips found hers as her body quaked. He swallowed her gasp as her pussy began clenching hard, squeezing the fingers inside her as a powerful orgasm took hold.

"Christ," Blake said from between her legs, his fingers biting into her thighs hard as he lapped at her. As he continued to lick her, Mac released the rope securing her arms. The second her hands were free, she reached for him, desperation urging her on.

"I want to taste you," she murmured.

His hands went to his buckle, and Blake climbed to his feet. He pulled her from the rock wall and stood behind her, capturing her breasts in his hands as he guided her to her knees, aligning her mouth with Mac's cock. She watched Mac and Blake exchanged a knowing look, then Blake pulled her hair back, giving it a little tug until her mouth was wide open and ready for Mac's thick cock.

Mac unzipped his pants and released his cock. He stroked it, and when his eyes met hers, her skin warmed all over. The intimacy in what they were doing, the connection between them, made this fantasy that much more extraordinary.

Blake dropped to his knees behind her and held her against him. She caught the thin sheen of sweat on Mac's upper lip, a sign that he was coming unglued as he fed her his cock. Sucking him in and loving the feel of him, the taste of him in her mouth, she took him as deep as she could.

"Fuck," Blake said from behind, and then made a sound of delight as he slid his fingers between her legs to play with her.

As Blake rubbed her, Mac cupped her face and rocked his hips, his growl of pleasure scaring a flock of birds in a nearby tree and sending them into flight.

Ignoring the squawks around her, she stayed between Mac's legs, running her tongue along the length of him, wanting to give him the same pleasure he'd given her. She sucked at the tangy fluid dripping from the slit, eager to taste more of him. He pumped into her mouth, his thumbs gently brushing her cheeks. She grew slicker between her thighs, needing desperately to be filled.

"You are so fucking hot," Blake said, as he dipped his fingers into her, helping to remedy the bone-deep longing pulling at her. She moaned around a mouthful of cock and caught another silent exchange between Mac and his friend. Before she realized what was happening, she heard Blake release his zipper. Mac pulled his cock from her mouth, and a moment later, he gripped her shoulders and pulled her up.

"I want to be inside you when I come," he murmured, pressing a kiss to her mouth. She licked her lips and nodded, eager to feel his huge cock inside her. Mac gestured beyond her shoulder to Blake, who was still kneeling. "Now get back down on your knees and take Blake into your mouth while I fuck you properly."

She let loose a breathy moan, lust stealing almost every ounce of her strength as she thought about Mac fucking her while she sucked Blake.

"I take it you like that idea?" Mac asked, grinning as he brushed his thumbs over her nipples.

Before she could answer, Blake dragged her down, turning her until she faced him. He flattened himself out on his back and pulled her over him until her breasts were pressed against his chest. He pushed on her shoulders, and she slid down, until her mouth was aligned with his cock. Mac gripped her hips, positioning her onto all fours.

"Jesus Christ," Mac said as she opened her body to him.

Mac rubbed his hand over her body, and after she listened to him sheathe himself, she wiggled until she could feel him breach her opening. She stole a glance at Blake before she took him into her mouth. He growled and powered his hips upward at the same time Mac drove into her. Three bodies came together as one, each giving and taking, sharing openly and honestly as they rocked her vanilla world. Good God, she'd never experienced anything quite so hedonistic, so incredibly passionate and real, in her entire life.

Even though she swore she wasn't going to get emotionally involved, her heart squeezed, knowing Mac had purposely set this scenario up for her. Truthfully, even though there had always been another side of her, one that wanted to explore numerous fantasies, she couldn't quite believe how far she'd come since stepping foot off the plane. But knowing she was under Mac's care, that he was there to watch over her as he guided her on her journey of self-discovery, filled her with a new kind of freedom.

She licked Blake's cock and cried Mac's name as he pounded into her with hot, hard strokes that stole the air from her lungs. He slowed long enough for her to catch her breath, easy, measured strokes that soothed as well as excited, then suddenly pulled back to the tip and sank balls-deep. Tension grew in her body as Mac and Blake fulfilled one of her deepest, darkest desires, but she didn't want to climax, didn't want this moment to ever end.

"I'm right there," Blake said, his voice like a rough caress as he gripped her hair. His cock thickened in her mouth, and she pulled back, letting him release on her breasts.

Mac growled, his fingers tightening on her hips. She knew he was close, nearing the breaking point but purposefully holding back. He was waiting for her.

He pumped harder, and heat suffused her body. As he drove her higher and higher, he angled his hips for deeper thrusts. Mac's hand slipped between their bodies, the rough pad of his fingers rubbing her clit.

"Oh, my God! Yessss…" Her breath grew shallow, and she leaned forward, pressing Blake's cock between her breasts as she tumbled over the edge of ecstasy. Blinding pleasure raced through her, and Blake wrapped his arms around her, holding her close as she rode out the pulsating waves.

"Son of a bitch!" Mac's forehead fell between her

shoulders, his breath hot against her sweat-slicked flesh.

Her muscles continued to clench around Mac's cock and she exhaled a whimper of relief as her body trembled in bliss. He slid his palm over her, spread his fingers, and rubbed them over the lips of her pussy, wringing one last spasm from her aching core and another cry of pleasure from her lips. He stilled inside her. A moan of pleasure erupted from deep within his chest, filling her as he let go.

He completely collapsed on top of her, his hands circling her waist to hold on tight. She reveled in the feel of his weight holding her down, and thought about how nice it felt to be held by him.

"Sweetheart," Mac murmured into her ear. "You're going to be the death of me."

Her heart took that moment to tighten, because being with him like this was unlike anything she'd ever experienced before. It was true—Mac was the kind of guy every girl wanted, and she was no exception, which had her realizing that when he got bored and this sexual adventure was over, walking away was going to be harder than she ever anticipated.

Chapter Seven

When Mac finally got his breathing under control, he inched back, gripped Jess by the waist, and eased his cock out of her. He lifted her to her feet, the intimacy in what they'd just done creating a deeper bond between them. One he had a feeling she understood every bit as much as he did.

He offered her an apologetic grin and said, "Ah, sorry about interrupting your stretches."

She nibbled her bottom lip, a sexy grin on her mouth. "I'm pretty sure what we did here was better than any workout."

"Still," he said as he brushed his thumb over her flushed cheeks, soaking in her beauty. "If you want to finish, I'd love to join you."

She tucked her hair behind her ears. "I think I had enough of a workout," she murmured.

He looked past Jess's shoulder to see Blake climb back

into his pants. Mac gave a curt nod to his friend, and when he returned it, Jess spun to face the other man. Mac pulled her closer against him as Blake finished dressing. The other man fastened his belt, and then put his hands on Jess's shoulders. Even though they'd just shared her, possession raced through Mac and he tried not to flinch as Blake dropped a kiss onto her forehead.

He glanced at Mac. "I can see why you'd never want to let this one get away," he said. "She's special." He cocked his head, a warm smile on his face when he continued with, "And the pleasure was all mine." He drove a blade of grass between his lips and walked away, leaving Mac alone with Jess.

A frown pulled at her lips when she turned back to him, and he nudged her chin. "Hey, what's wrong?"

"You told Blake I was special?"

"Sure. I want everyone to know you're mine."

Surprise moved over her face. "Oh."

"Come on." He grabbed her hand.

"Where we going now?"

"To shower," he said. He cast her a devious glance. "Then we have lots of time to play before I have to attend to my ranch duties."

She arched a questioning brow, but he didn't bother to explain that later, he'd be teaching a crowd how to make a lasso and hog-tie cattle and that he planned to use her as his student. Since she wasn't one for loud crowds, he felt it was best to keep his plan under wraps for the time being. No need in scaring her off.

A warm, comfortable silence fell over them as Mac captured her hand and walked her back to her room for a shower. They stepped inside her suite, and after washing each other under the warm spray, he wrapped her in a towel and said, "How would you like to grab some climbing gear and take a different way up the mountain?

"I would love that."

"We can have breakfast at the top."

Her towel dropped an inch to expose her cleavage. "How is it you always seem to know what I'm thinking?"

Instead of answering, his glance moved over the lush swell of her breasts. He tamped down his swelling cock and slapped her bare ass. "Ahh, you'd better get dressed or we'll never get out of here."

She yelped and hurried into a fresh set of clothes. Thirty minutes later, after arranging for another picnic breakfast and gathering his climbing gear, Mac guided her toward the smallest, safest mountain. Since she'd never rock climbed before, Mac hooked her to the safety gear and gave her a run-through. He took the lead, and she followed from behind. He glanced over his shoulder, keeping a close eye on her progress, pleased to see her lovely face in concentration as she followed his instructions to a *T*. They made better progress than he expected, and before he knew it, they were standing at the peak. His chest swelled when he took in the smile on her face. He loved seeing her so happy.

"Thank you for bringing me here." She breathed in the air and looked at the ranch in the distance. "It's so beautiful."

"So are you," Mac said, coming up behind her. He slipped his arm around her waist, and she exhaled slowly.

"I love it here," she whispered, pointing to the ground. "Right here, this very spot. I never want to leave."

He spun her around to face him. "Maybe you'd like to

stay longer."

When she frowned and looked down, his stomach tightened. He put his hand under her chin and lifted it. "What is it? What aren't you telling me?"

"I just…I don't want to talk about it."

"Hey, it's me. You can tell me anything."

Her lashes fluttered rapidly. "I know."

"So tell me."

"It's just… the thoughts of going back…to my studio."

"You're not happy there?"

"No, just the opposite. I love it there, but my business is failing. I don't have the marketing skill you do, and if I can't figure out how to bring in more clients, I'll have to close the doors."

"Let me help."

She shook her head quickly. "No, I didn't mean… I'm not telling you this because… Please don't think…"

"You know what I think?" he whispered. "Maybe the food can wait a little longer."

"I like the way you think," she murmured as his mouth closed over hers.

After another round of lovemaking and breakfast on the hilltop, Jess found herself standing outside a dusty sheep pen alongside other guests at the ranch while Mac walked the outer edge with a rope, teaching all the onlookers how to make a lasso. As she watched him loop the rope, a shiver moved through her, her thoughts traveling back to earlier that morning. She couldn't help but wonder if that was the same rope he'd used to tie her up.

As she reminisced about all the naughty things he and Blake had done to her, he proceeded to spin the rope in the air, enthralling the crowd with his cowboy tricks as the sheep grazed at the far end of the pen. A noise sounded from behind her, and she looked over her shoulder to catch a glimpse of Jag, his powerful legs wrapped around a huge black stallion. Behind him, she spotted Alix, one of the other girls who boarded the small plane with her and Julia, and a few other ranch guests. Jess could only assume Jag's afternoon chore was to give horseback riding lessons. Even though she'd never been on a horse, she'd love to try it out. Perhaps she'd ask Mac to give her a private lesson later on in the week.

She turned her attention back to Mac. As she watched him look over the crowd, it became glaringly apparent that people were drawn to him because of his honesty, openness, and enthusiastic personality. Even though he was currently putting on a show, he seemed genuine, like he really cared about the people under his charge. His sincerity came out in his actions, the way he spoke and the way he listened. Her thoughts turned to her business, and she knew she could definitely learn a thing or two about engaging clients enough to come back to the studio simply from watching him. But their time was ending soon…

Beside her, the two women who'd been with Blake earlier started giggling and talking quietly about Mac as he walked around the roping pen to showcase his lasso skills. Jess tried to concentrate, but the women beside her continued to chat quietly, making remarks about Mac's hard body and how they'd like to be the ones roped and tied by the sexy ranch owner.

A knot tightened in Jess's stomach, and she felt an un-wise pang of jealousy. She and Mac might have been indulg-ing in each other sexually, but the vivacious women in the short shorts and low-cut halter-tops were probably the types he'd usually gone for in the past. He'd said he kept up with her, but she'd seen him in some of the newspapers and on television at various charity events. He always had a super-model-pretty woman on his arm. A wild guy like him could resist that kind of temptation for only so long. And when he did, she'd be a thing of the past. She swallowed the knot in her throat and reminded herself that she didn't want more, anyway.

Keep telling yourself that; you might believe it in a year or so. No. The last thing she wanted was to end up alone and lonely like her mother. This week was simply about freeing herself sexually.

I've certainly done that.

Her thoughts were interrupted when Mac asked for a volunteer. The women beside her both started jumping up and down. Jess worked to shrink back into the crowd, but Mac would have none of that. He pointed to her, and before she knew what was happening, Blake had her by the elbow and was guiding her inside the pen.

His smile was slow. "Looks like it's your lucky day."

Butterflies swarmed in her stomach, but the second she looked into Mac's eyes and he gave her a warm, reassuring smile, she found herself relaxing.

Despite that, she whispered, "You're so going to pay for this."

He grinned and exchanged a private look with her.

"That's what I'm counting on."

Returning to professional mode, he said in a sexy twang, "Okay, darlin', you take the rope in your hand, swing ever so easy like this, then release it." He tossed the rope, and it slipped around the neck of a sheep. He walked toward the animal, gathering the rope in a loop. He released it from the sheep's neck and said, "And before you know it, you'll be roping yourself some cattle."

Jess planted her feet in the dirt and followed his instruction, twirling the rope in the air, but when she let it go, it fell short of her target, catching nothing but a circle of dry soil. With stubborn determination, she tried again...and then again, dragging the rope through the dirt and soiling her hands and clothes as she collected it to try yet again. On her fifth turn, Mac tucked in behind her. He pressed his hard body to hers, making any sort of concentration impossible.

"Like this, darlin'," he murmured into her ear as he closed his hand over hers, showing her how to hold the rope. Was it actually necessary that he spoon up to her like this? She didn't think so. Well, two could play that game. She wiggled her ass, a slight movement that only he'd be able to detect, and a low growl crawled out of his throat.

"Cut it out," he warned.

"Or what?"

Before he could answer, Blake called out to the crowd, inviting everyone into the pen to try their hands at roping. Mac inched back, and when the two girls who were whispering about him earlier stepped up and asked for his help, he turned his attention to them. She pushed down another twinge of jealousy. This was part of his chores. And she had no ownership of him.

Jess took that time to slip from the arena, leaving him to his duties. As he entertained guests and worked to make their ranch experiences memorable, she remembered what Mac had said about extreme situations. As she mulled that over, thinking about the extreme measures he'd taken with her, she couldn't help but wonder if he was still taking them with other guests. If Blake asked Mac to participate in something like they did on the mountain, would he? Oh boy, she was in trouble, because she didn't like how that made her feel.

Mac cast her a questioning glance; she smiled and made a motion indicating she was going for a drink, a half truth. While she was thirsty, what she really needed was a moment of reprieve to get herself together and tamp down the jealousy eating at her. She needed to put some distance between them, think about what was happening to her, what she was feeling.

Deciding to go on a self-directed tour, she walked around the saloon, enjoying a moment of quiet as she strolled past the pool toward the lake at the far end of the ranch. She took a moment of reflection, working to get her head on straight where Mac was concerned. She made her way inside the saloon and ordered an iced tea. Taking a seat by the window, she sipped on it and watched Mac twirl and toss a rope off in the distance. Laughter rose from the corral as Blake worked his magic, amusing the crowd. Jess's thoughts drifted back to what happened among the three of them earlier that morning and how the two gorgeous men had thoroughly *entertained* her.

But that's all it was—entertainment.

She sat there for a long time thinking, and eventually the door swung open again, but she didn't need to turn to know it was Mac. Sexual energy arced between them like a pair of Tesla coils, alerting her to his presence long before she saw him. Her heart thundered, her body warming all over as he stepped up to her.

The sexy grin he gave her when his eyes latched onto hers made her forget everything except this man and his ability to turn her inside out with a smile.

Her glance moved over his clothes, which were also soiled from grass and dirt, and he reached out and brushed his thumb over her cheek, his look playful, sexy.

"Hey, cowgirl," he murmured, his slow, lazy grin like a seductive caress. "Why don't you help me rustle up a bar of soap?"

She tamped down her emotions and gave herself a hard lecture, reminding herself this was temporary. Right now was the time to make the most of every second she had left here, not dwell on how it was going to end.

She climbed to her feet and followed him to the lodge. Instead of heading toward her suite, he led her in another direction. A few minutes later, she found herself inside his bedroom.

He ushered her in, and a shiver moved down her spine when the lock clicked into place behind her. A strong hand slipped around her waist, and her body warmed as he pulled her close.

"I've been thinking about you all afternoon. How about that shower?" he whispered. Then he tugged her T-shirt from her shorts. His mouth dropped to her neck, and as he kissed her, she realized how easy he was to be with, how much she wanted him again. And even though it might not be in her best interest—getting too personal would only prove to make it harder when she walked away—she was curious to know more about Tyler Mackenzie the man, not Wildman Mac, the bad boy.

She inched away from him, perusing his personal space in an attempt to understand him better. "So this is how you live on weekends," she said, moving about his room and running her fingers over his sparse belongings. She noticed his open laptop and phone on his bureau.

He frowned. "Most of the time I come here to relax, but sometimes work beckons—some last-minute problem that I can't ignore—which means I can't completely unplug."

Like her dad, he probably worked all the time, even when he was out here in the middle of nowhere. She could never be with a guy who couldn't set work aside, even for a weekend.

When she went quiet, thinking about how much she liked him, all the things they'd been doing together, he touched her chin. "Hey, is everything okay?"

"I was just wondering. What we did this morning, with Blake, is that the kind of thing you guys do a lot? Not that it's really any of my business…I was just curious."

"I told you I'd never lie to you, Jess, so yes, we've done that before." He pulled her in tight and pushed her hair off her forehead. "But this time, it wasn't about us, it was about you."

"Because of my journal."

"Because I wanted to give you everything you've ever wanted, Jess." His thumb brushed her cheek and warmth moved through her. He briefly closed his eyes and exhaled hard. "If you want the full truth, sharing you damn near killed me."

Her stomach fluttered as understanding dawned. Her

mind recalled the clench of his jaw, the almost tortured look on his face, the way he took possession of her, claiming her mouth, her body. Sharing had been hard for him, but he did it for her. Oh God.

"Mac…"

"If it's okay with you, I don't ever want another man's hands on your body."

She should be angry by his possessiveness, but it only made her want him more.

Mac pulled his shirt off, and her brain shifted directions. She took in his rippling muscles and the heat in his eye when they met hers.

"I need you naked, darlin.'"

Her hand went to the button on her shorts, and before she knew it, the rest of the day was lost to soap and sex with the hottest cowboy she knew…a guy—despite knowing they could never be together because he wasn't the settling-down type—she was seriously falling for him.

Chapter Eight

Sitting in the saloon, Mac took a sip of his beer and stole a glance at the beautiful woman beside him. Conversation between his two best friends, Coop and Jag, and the girls they'd invited for the week took place around him, but he paid little mind to them. All of his attention was focused on Jess and the emotions she brought out in him.

Four days had passed since she'd first stepped foot on the ranch, and while they'd done so much together, there were still so many things he wanted to do with her. Even though she'd opened up to him on many levels, he sensed she was holding back from giving herself to him fully.

She talked quietly with the others, every now and then casting him a glance—her eyes an intriguing contradiction of mystery and promise. His heart pounded harder in his chest as he looked at her, and it occurred to him how much he wanted—needed—her alone. Just to kiss her, hold her, feel her in his arms. He remained quiet, listening to the sweet lilt of her voice. Her hand dropped to his knee. Whether her move had been intended as casual or suggestive, Mac's reaction was the same. Possession.

Tamara's boots echoed dully on the plank floor as she stepped up to the table to replenish their drinks. Mac tipped the bottle and swallowed, welcoming the cool liquid as it reached the dryness in his throat, but knew there was only one thing that would help hydrate him—climbing between Jess's legs and drinking in her sweetness as he gave her pleasure.

Jesus Christ, he needed to be inside her. Everywhere. Now.

His chair scraped across the floor as he pushed back from the table and stood. All eyes turned to him. Making no attempt at discretion, and needing them to be together, he pulled Jess to her feet and said, "We need to go."

Jess nodded. He hauled her close, and as her warm body collided with his, he excused them from the table.

With a single-minded determination, he guided her through the saloon and out the back door. He cut through the barn and caught the question in her eyes when he grabbed a blanket and the backpack he'd dropped in there earlier that day. His intentions had been to make love to her in the hayloft tonight, but the sky was so clear and beautiful, and she loved nature so much, he thought he'd take her to her favorite spot instead.

Guided by the moon and stars on the warm summer night, they walked along the footpath until they reached the peak of the mountain. He led her to the grassy edge, to where they'd been doing yoga every morning.

He dropped the blanket, stepped behind her, and wrapped his arms around her small body as they glanced at the majestic view. Off in the distance, a horse whinnied, and the fresh scent of hay filled the air. They stayed like that for a long time, just holding each other, enjoying the feel of their bodies pressed together, and basking in the warm familiarity of each other as they stared into the moonlit night.

Jess exhaled slowly and finally broke the quiet when she said, "I could stay here forever."

His heart leaped at her softly spoken confession. He spun her to face him, looked deep into her eyes, and realized he didn't care where he was, as long as he was with her. "You can come here every weekend with me."

Doubt clouded her eyes, and her brow furrowed. "Mac," she began, but he pressed his lips to hers, swallowing her protest. He refused to let anything spoil this precious moment.

"Tonight is for feeling, not thinking," he whispered between kisses, determined to eradicate her worries and prove to her once and for all how much they belonged together. He pulled her tighter and lifted her onto his hips, securing her small frame with one hand.

He could feel her heart thumping with a beat that spurred him into action. When her body relaxed against his, he ran his thumb over her bottom lip, his cock aching for something far more intimate.

"Baby, I want you so much. I want to be inside you." His hand left her mouth. He trailed it lower and lower until he reached her ass. He stroked lightly, letting her know his intentions when he said, "Everywhere."

She moved against him, giving him a look that tightened his balls against his body.

"Everywhere?" she asked, a moan catching in her throat as her eyes met his.

He dropped her lower on his hips until his cock pushed against her ass. "Yeah, everywhere," he confirmed.

Her dark lashes fluttered. Christ, he loved watching her blossom before him, loved watching her become the sensual, adventurous woman she always wanted to be.

"Tell me something, sweetheart."

"What?"

"If I slide my hand inside your shorts, will I find you hot for me?"

"Always," she whispered.

He shifted his body, letting her slide to her feet. She moved against him impatiently. Mac ran his hands along her back, and when she wet her bottom lip with a quick swipe of her tongue, it fueled the lust inside him. He pulled her T-shirt from the waistband of her shorts and slipped his hand underneath the cotton, reveling in the feel of her soft stomach beneath his hands. He brushed her flesh and stroked higher until he reached the underside of her breasts. He freed one nipple from her bra, and she pushed against him as he scraped his thumb over her hard pebbles.

"Pinch my nipples." Her raspy voice and bold words sent a barrage of erotic sensations through him as everything inside urged him to rip her clothes from her body and take her hard and fast. Christ, no matter how many times he made love to her, he knew he'd never be able to assuage his hunger where she was concerned.

He sucked in air and worked to center himself, but when she straddled his leg and rubbed herself against him, it rattled him right to his very core. He slipped a hand into her shorts, and when he felt her, hot and wet against his fingers—for him, just for him—need stole every ounce of his strength.

He gripped her panties and air left her lungs in a rush when he pushed them to the side. He ran his thumb over her clit and moaned out loud as her nub swelled with heated blood at his touch.

Voices drifted up from the compound, but he ignored them. Nothing existed, nothing else mattered except the woman in his arms. He slid his fingers over her silken folds, her warmth easing the path as he pushed a finger into her core.

"Oh, God, yes," she cried out, her voice full of sultry invitation as it reverberated off the Rocky Mountains.

Primitive need urged him on, and he forced himself to breathe slowly. She placed her hand over his cock and rubbed him through his jeans. A gust of wind came out of nowhere, carrying the last of his restraint with it.

Overcome with the things he felt for her, the things she made him feel without even trying, his mouth watered for a taste of her. He dragged her to the ground. Her eyes shimmered with sensuality as she positioned herself in the center of the blanket and widened her legs, welcoming him to her body. He growled and climbed over her. Pinning her beneath him, he took full possession of her mouth, kissing her hard enough to leave her lips swollen and bruised. Her hands clawed at his clothes, tugging his T-shirt over his head. Feeling wild, crazy, and completely out of control, he inched away to pull it off his shoulders. When he caught the sultry way she looked at his chest, he went back on his heels.

"Get naked," he demanded, his body about to go up in a burst of flames.

"Mac," she said, a hesitation in her voice.

He gave her a perplexed frown. "What is it?"

"You asked if there was something I wanted to share with you. Something from my journal…"

His blood burned hotter than ever; he was anxious to help her live out all her fantasies. "Tell me."

She nibbled her bottom lip and went quiet.

"Tell me, Jess," he said again.

She drew a deep breath and blurted out, "I…well…after watching those dancers, I want to dance…*strip*…for you."

He exhaled slowly, his nostrils flaring, and giving her the little push she both needed and wanted, he said, "Stand up."

Her body trembled visibly as she climbed to her feet, and Mac sat up to take it all in. She began swaying her hips, moving to the beat in her own head as she slowly, torturously, gripped the hem of her T-shirt to toy with it. He growled, and when he shifted his cock, a small smile pulled at her mouth. The sight of his erection seemed to urge her on. She removed her shirt, and then her hands went to the button on her shorts. She wiggled her hips as she released it, and when she slid them down her legs, it was all he could do not to pin her beneath him and fuck her hard. But he knew she needed to do this, for him, and for her. Standing there in nothing but a bra and skimpy panties, she ran her hands over her body in a seductive manner that would turn any sane person mad.

Mac sank back onto his elbow, enjoying her foreplay. *She's so goddamn sexy*. His cock ached. Groaning, he brushed his hand over his jeans to reposition his hard-on a second time. She turned her back to him, tipping that sweet ass of hers in the air. Christ, did she know he was an ass man and that if she kept that up, he'd have no choice but to put an end to this and fuck that backside of hers once and for all?

Jess turned, undulating her body. God, she was so

beautiful and sexy he couldn't take his eyes off her. She released her bra and when her breasts fell free, he nearly sobbed.

His blood flowed hot and heavy in his veins as she danced for him, and a low growl of longing rumbled in his throat. Christ, he knew she was enjoying herself, enjoying performing for him, but he could no longer sit there and take this kind of torture.

He stood, captured her hips, and hauled her to him, crushing her body to his as she pressed against him. The need and desire in her eyes as she looked at him damn near rendered him senseless.

He inched back, and wanting to push her a little further, he said, "Touch yourself for me."

"Mac," she whimpered breathlessly.

His voice dropped an octave when he said, "I'm not asking."

She watched him carefully.

"Show me how you touch yourself," he said, urging her to shed the last of her inhibitions. "Show me what you do in bed at night after you finish writing out one of your secret fantasies."

They exchanged a long, knowing look. She gave him a slow, sexy smile, her body shaking with unabashed hunger. She placed her hands on her breasts and pinched her nipples.

"That's a girl," he said.

Her hands trailed lower, and heat flooded him as she removed her panties and dipped her fingers inside her pussy. She cried out in bliss, and as her body came alive before him, he thought he'd died and gone to heaven.

Her mouth went slack, and her breathing changed as her

fingers moved swiftly over her wet slit. Growing bolder, her eyes never left his as she touched herself, creating a deeper connection between them and triggering a craving like he'd never before experienced.

Desperate to see her pink sweetness, he grabbed her and laid her out on the blanket. Sweat dotted his brow as she widened her legs. His body ached to join with hers, to lose itself in the heat between her legs when she opened herself up so nicely, baring herself to him on so many levels.

He dropped between her legs and as he sat there teetering on the edge, tension rose in him, the sweet scent of her arousal reaching his nostrils and making him mad with the need to fuck her. Breathing became difficult as he slid his hands over her soft flesh until his fingers joined with hers.

"Yes," she cried out as he sank a finger inside her wet heat.

"Jesus." He was sure he'd never get used to her tightness. His cock throbbed. He trembled with the urge to touch her, to taste her, to prove to her once and for all they belonged together. He bent forward and pressed his mouth to her. Her hips came off the ground, and she fisted her hands in his hair, her body trembling all over.

Her walls squeezed his fingers, her body screaming for release. He punched up the pressure, added a second finger, pumping them in and out of her, his tongue going to her sensitive clit to draw small circles. Her hips rose and bucked against his face. He pushed another thick finger inside. His cock throbbed as she gripped his shoulders and cried out his name.

He lightly brushed the bundle of nerves inside her as she continued to ride his mouth and fingers, her body coming unglued as she chased release.

"That's my girl," he said. "Take what you need."

A moment later, she shuddered a breath, her body succumbing to the pleasure with a hot flow of release. As she came for him, he licked every last drop of her sweetness. When she stopped trembling, he went back on his heels, and in a voice that wasn't quite steady, he said, "I need you, baby. I need you so goddamn much."

"Please," she begged.

Taking her by surprise, he flipped her over. When a gasp sounded in her throat, he slid a hand down her back until he reached her crevice. He stroked her lightly, and with the need to mark her—everywhere—his voice came out fractured and broken when he said, "Tonight, I need to be inside you here, sweetheart." He tore off the rest of his clothes and tucked them under her hips to raise her beautiful ass in the air.

He ran his hands over her soft cheeks. "I've never…" Her voice came out so low, so soft, he had to strain to hear her.

He loved how honest and open they could be with each other. "But you want to, don't you, darlin'?" When a whimper caught in her throat, he said, "It's part of your fantasy, isn't it?" He guessed at that last part, but he had a feeling he knew her better than she did herself.

Nervous excitement laced her voice, filling him with a new kind of need when she nodded and said quietly, "Yes."

He reached into his backpack and pulled out a tube of lubricant, wanting to prepare her properly as he claimed her and marked her in a way she'd never been marked by another. He squirted a generous amount onto her back, and watched it trickle over her curves and between her ass cheeks.

She wiggled, and he couldn't believe how lucky he was to be here with her, how blessed he was that this beautiful, sweet, kind, and compassionate woman was gifting him with her body in such an intimate way.

He ran the lubricant over her and gently pushed a finger inside, determined to take it slow and make this new experience good for her. Offering her only an inch at a time and letting her get used to the fullness, he spent a long time stretching her, playing with her back passage until she began moving, rocking her hips in an urgent manner.

"You're not ready yet, sweetheart," he growled, barely able to keep it together himself.

Tension built inside him, but he forced himself to stay calm, even going so far as to practice a few of those breathing exercises she taught him. He spent a few more moments introducing his fingers to her crevice, and when she pushed backward, demanding more, he gripped his cock and stroked it over her soft slit.

With her passion flaring hot, he quickly sheathed himself, lubed up, and positioned himself at her entrance. He took his time entering her, and when her fingers curled in the blanket, he stilled.

"Am I hurting you?"

"A little," she said honestly. "But I want this, Mac. I want you inside me like this."

He slipped a finger around her body and brushed her clit. When she starting moaning in pleasure, he pushed his cock in another inch, a gentle thrust that drove him past her opening. She groaned and moved against him. When her body finally relaxed and fully opened for him, he slipped all the way inside her.

"Jesus," he moaned.

She began rocking, moving against him. He gripped her hips and held her tight, unable to get enough of her as they joined together in a new and beautiful way.

His heart squeezed, and he closed his eyes in distress, his breathing changing, as she met and welcomed each and every push. He bit back a growl, knowing he wasn't going to last long. She continued to move against him, and he dug his fingers into her hips, following the motion of her beautiful body.

When she began to tremble, he reached around her and stroked her clit. Once, twice, and then he felt a shudder move through her. Their moans of pleasure mingled, and blood flowed hot and heavy in his veins when she let go. As she gave herself over to him completely, the world around him seemed to disappear.

He drove deep and stilled, his own orgasm hitting so fast and hard it was all he could do to drag in air. Blinding pleasure swamped him, and he stayed deep inside her until he depleted himself completely.

He fell over her back, his cock still buried inside her as they both worked to get their breathing under control. After a moment, he eased out of her and rolled and cleaned them both off with some wipes he'd brought. Then he drew her close, every feeling he had for her so close to the surface.

"Are you okay, baby?"

She snuggled closer, tucking her head into the curve of his neck. "I'm fine. That was…I mean. Wow."

"Yeah, 'wow' pretty much sums it up." He tucked her in tighter and glanced at the girl he'd spent half his life in love with.

She smiled, a bevy of emotions in her eyes as she shifted closer. She ran her hands along his chest, and there was a peculiar hitch in her voice when she murmured, "I could really get used to this."

Mac's heart pounded in his chest, the uncertainly in her voice triggering alarm bells. Sure, they'd been having fun. This hedonistic week was about letting go and exploring each other. But when it was over, what if she no longer wanted him in her life? What if, to her, this sexual adventure was simply that...a sexual adventure?

That wouldn't do. That wouldn't do at all. He hadn't lied. She was his. They hadn't been together long, but she'd already wrapped herself around his heart.

Chapter Nine

For the next three days, Jess spent every waking hour with Mac, and every sleeping hour, too. He loved how she'd finally opened up to him, even telling him about her failing business. Mac wanted to help her revive her yoga studio the same way he helped everyone he cared about, but he knew she wasn't asking for a handout from his company—which made him want to help her all the more.

Sitting in his room, he dialed his assistant and thought about all the things they'd done, from hiking, karaoke, and swimming, to making love every chance they had. Soon enough she'd be boarding a plane, and he hoped she was willing to give him a chance when they returned to the real world, hoped that she believed in him, believed that he was a one-woman kind of guy who was serious about playing for keeps. As he thought of the alternative, his heart tightened, because now that he had a taste of life with her in it, he couldn't imagine his future without her.

He stole a glance at his watch. Damn, he was running late. He was supposed to meet Jess in her room after he finished up with his ranch chores—but he had one very important matter to take care of before he took her in his arms again.

After another glorious night with Mac, Jess stretched out on the mattress. Despite her best efforts, she couldn't fight her growing attraction to him. Even though this was supposed to be a brief affair where her emotions weren't involved, she genuinely liked everything about him, and she found herself opening up to him on all levels.

As she stirred awake, another thought hit. It was true that Mac had grown up, changed since their youth, which made her wonder if he really was interested in playing for keeps. But could he be the kind of guy who learned to unplug, like he said, or like her father, would he promise things and not deliver?

She reached for the man who'd come to mean so much to her. When her hand found air, she rolled over, only to find his side of the bed empty. Apprehension coiled in her stomach, because not only was the bed empty, the sheets were cold, a clear sign that he'd been gone for a long time.

Grabbing a sheet to cover herself, she climbed from the bed and checked the bathroom only to find that vacant, too. Wondering where he'd gone off to, she walked to her window. With the morning sun cresting the horizon, she pulled open her curtains, and her heart lodged somewhere in her throat when she caught a shirtless Mac coming out of the barn.

She narrowed her eyes, trying to figure out who was coming out behind him, but when she spotted Blake, also shirtless, a knot formed in her stomach. Were they both out there entertaining some woman, the same way they'd entertained her? When the two women she'd become so familiar with—the same two who'd taken over after her at the karaoke machine and had jumped at the opportunity for Mac to teach them roping skills—exited the barn, Jess drew in a breath and inched away from the window. Her mind reached, searching to make sense of what was happening. She dropped onto her bed, confusion morphing to anger. Hadn't she warned herself not to get too close to a guy who was always on the quest for the next exciting adventure? God, she never should have let herself believe they could have more. That he'd changed his ways. But the truth was, she knew from the beginning what she was getting herself into.

Jess grabbed her suitcase off the bench and tossed it on her bed, her heart aching as the sight of him with those two women reminded her what this was, and more importantly, what it wasn't. Her initial plan had been to have sex with Mac and walk away when it was over. She stole a glance at her clock and knew she couldn't just leave without saying good-bye. Truthfully, she should be grateful for all he'd given her, and she wanted to be the bigger person here.

But that was hard when her heart felt as if it had been ripped in two.

Suck it up. You can do this.

Before heading to the lobby to arrange for the next flight, she made her way to his room. She knocked quietly on his door and unease moved through her, worried that she wouldn't find him alone. He swung it open and a wide smile split Mac's somber face when he saw her. "You're awake," he said quietly. He kicked off his boots and came toward her, then his steps slowed, his glance moving over her face. "What's wrong?"

"I wanted to say good-bye."

"Good-bye?" He ran a hand through his hair. "What the hell?"

"I know our time is up, Mac."

"Like hell it is!"

She looked at his still-bare chest. "I saw you coming from the barn with Blake and those two girls."

He scrubbed his hand through his hair, looking at her as though she'd sprouted a second head, then his brows shot up. "Oh, shit." He pulled her into his room and shut the door. "Jess," he began. "You're the only girl I want in my life."

"But I saw…"

"What did you really see?"

"I just saw you, Blake, those girls…no shirts."

He pressed his fingers to hers. "Eleanor foaled last night. She went early. Blake came to get me. You were sleeping so soundly I didn't want to wake you, and I thought I'd be back before you woke up."

Taken aback, she said, "Oh."

"She had complications last time, so I wanted to be there with her. Sweetheart, believe me, the only one I want to give an authentic cowboy experience to is you. I wasn't in the loft with anyone. Neither was Blake. He sat up with me all night. And our shirts, well, they got dirty."

"But I saw those girls, and I just…"

He smiled. "I'm not saying Blake hadn't been with them earlier in the night. I'm certain he was, but while they slept, he helped me keep watch over Eleanor."

Feeling suddenly horrible for second-guessing this man, a man who'd done so much for her over the week, a man who was protective, sweet, genuine, and caring, and would go to great lengths for those he cared about, she asked, "Is she okay?"

The warmth in his smile set her heart racing. "Yeah, so is her little filly."

"She had a girl?"

"Yeah, she's beautiful."

She felt her whole world shift, the sensitive side of Mac filling her heart with love. God, there really was more to this man than met the eyes. She took a moment to think back to her first day on the ranch, when he'd asked for her submission, for her to put herself in his hands. Now she knew why. He wanted to push her so he could help her open up, inside the bedroom and out. She might never have done that if she wasn't under his guidance, his care.

Swallowing the knot punching into her throat, she whispered, "You're a good man, Mac."

She detected a glimmer of vulnerability in the depth of his eyes when he said quietly, "I'd do anything for those I care about."

"I know."

"I'm sorry I wasn't there when you woke. I thought I'd be back in time, which is why I didn't leave a note. I had some business to take care of."

Just then the sound of a fax coming in caught her attention.

"Right, business first," she said, sadness invading her gut.

Mac moved to the fax and his body tensed. He shifted so she couldn't see what he was looking at.

"Mac?" she asked.

"Never business first, Jess."

Confused, she asked, "What's going on?"

"I didn't want you to know."

She put her hand over her stomach. "Didn't want me to know what?"

He held a sheet of paper out for her to see. "I didn't want you to know this, but I can't let you think I'd put business over you."

She shook her head, hardly able to believe she was looking at a business campaign for her studio. "I told you I didn't…I wasn't looking…"

"I know that. Believe me I know that, but I wanted to do this. For you. Yoga is important to you so it's important to me, too."

Her heart soared, amazed that he'd do this for her, but of course, she couldn't afford such a campaign. "You know I can't allow you to do this, right?"

"Which is why I didn't want you to know."

Her throat tightened, and tears pooled in her eyes. "Mac, you didn't have to do this for me."

"I know I didn't have to. I want to."

"I can't afford it, and I'm not about to take something for free."

He grabbed her hand, dragged her closer. "Who said anything about free?"

She caught the playful look in his eyes. "What are you suggesting?"

"There are other ways to settle a debt."

Her insides warmed with the love she felt for this man. "You're a very naughty boy, you know."

He scooped her up and tossed her on the bed. "Then I guess it's a good thing I found a very naughty girl."

"A very good thing, indeed," she agreed.

"And just for the record, Jess, I told you before I would always be honest with you. So when I told you I'd never put business above those I love, I meant it."

"You…you love me?"

"Of course I love you!"

He climbed over her, holding her captive beneath him, like he was afraid she might flee. As he kissed her with tenderness and passion, she knew the boy from her past had grown into an incredible man, one she couldn't wait to spend the rest of her life with.

"And I love you, Tyler Mackenzie." she said, letting him know she had no desire to run away from him again, and every intention of bedding down with him today, tomorrow, and forever. "I'm pretty sure I always have."

Epilogue

Six months later

As the plane came to a rolling stop, Jess turned to look at the man who'd stolen her heart, the man she'd recently married and just honeymooned with in Jamaica. A big smile split his handsome face as he unbuckled his seat belt and turned her way.

"Are you ready?" he asked, looking more excited than a small boy on Christmas morning.

She eyed him skeptically. "I'm not sure." Honestly, she had no idea what he was up to, but was sure it had something to do with the words he whispered in her ear in bed last night as their honeymoon came to an end.

We've been fulfilling all your fantasies, now it's time to fulfill one of mine.

He dropped a soft kiss onto her mouth, and her heart soared. God, she was so crazy in love with him that sometimes it was impossible to breathe. Life had been full of wonderful surprises with Mac, and he always kept her on her toes. Truthfully, she loved his energy as much as he loved her calmness. While they might be opposites, they complemented each other perfectly.

She looked past his shoulders to take in the skim of snow on the ranch. Her hand went to her chest. "Mac, it's so gorgeous." She hadn't been back since last summer, and before they returned home to Nova Scotia, to her flourishing yoga studio thanks to Mac's help, he said he wanted to take her to the ranch for a special surprise. Something that involved his fantasies, she assumed.

The plane door opened and she found ranch hand Blake coming on board, winter coats and boots for both of them in hand. As she thought about the way Mac had enlisted the man's help to fulfill one of her many fantasies, her heart warmed. What warmed her even more was knowing Mac hadn't wanted to share her. He only had because he wanted to give her everything she'd ever desired.

"Blake," Mac said, as they exchanged handshakes. "Is everything in place?"

"All set," Blake said, handing over the winter gear as he tossed a smile Jess's way. "Hey Jess," he greeted, and placed a soft kiss on her cheek. Mac cast him a warning glare and Blake laughed. He held his hands palms-up. "I know. I know. She's all yours," he said and Jess laughed along with him.

Grumbling and tugging Jess close to show possession, Mac helped her into her gear, pulled on his own, and ushered her off the plane. Eyes wide, she glanced around to take in the snow-dusted dude ranch. It was beautiful in the summer, but words couldn't even begin to describe how cozy and romantic it felt in the winter.

A cool breeze moved over her face and she shivered.

Mac rubbed her arms. "Come on. Let's get you out of the cold."

They started toward the lodge, Blake by their side, but then Mac said, "Thanks for everything Blake. We'll catch up with you at dinner."

Blake nodded and disappeared inside the lodge while Mac turned her toward the mountain.

"Where are we going?"

Instead of answering, he pulled a handkerchief from his pocket and placed it over her eyes. Her pulse leaped, but she wasn't about to protest because she trusted Mac with her body, heart, and soul.

"I told you I have a surprise for you."

He held her tightly as he led her up the mountain, and a short while later, he stopped and whispered in her ear. "Ready?"

"I'm ready," she said, excitement building in her.

He pulled the kerchief off and she stood at the top of the mountain, the same spot she'd said she never wanted to leave. A spot where Mac had made sweet love to her. Before her stood a quaint cottage, puffs of smoke coming from the chimney.

"Mac?" she asked.

"Six months ago you stood on that exact spot and told me you never wanted to leave here, remember?"

"I remember."

"I built this for you. So you can come here in the summer or the winter, to the exact spot where we fell in love."

"I think I was in love with you long before that, Mac."

He grinned. "Yeah, me, too."

"It's beautiful." She put her arms around him and gave him a long, loving kiss. "Thank you."

"Now, about my fantasy…"

She laughed. "I knew there had to be a catch."

He grabbed her hand, pushed the door open and scooped her up to carry her over the threshold. Embers sparked in the hearth and the warmth of the fireplace washed over her. As she took in the sofa facing the fire, and the bedroom loft overhead, she shed her coat, her heart soaring with the love she felt for Mac.

"Here's the catch," he began. "No electricity. We've both been working so hard, and are so busy back home, we need time away. Now, when we come here, we can really unplug."

"I love it so much."

"That's my fantasy, sweetheart. Having you here, all to myself, the outside world unable to get in as I put all your needs first."

She cupped his cheeks. "You are the sweetest man in the world."

He touched her shirt. "And you, my darlin', are completely overdressed."

Acknowledgments

Huge thank you to the FOXY gals who had a piece in shaping this book. Rhonda Brant, Crystal Yawn, Danita Montes, Franci Neill, Chrissy Dryer and Debbie Watson.

About the Author

New York Times and *USA Today* bestselling author Cathryn Fox is a wife, mom, sister, daughter, and friend. She loves dogs, sunny weather, anything chocolate (she never says no to a brownie) pizza and red wine. Cathryn has two teenagers who keep her busy and a husband who is convinced he can turn her into a mixed martial arts fan. When not writing, Cathryn can be found laughing over lunch with friends, hanging out with her kids, or watching a big action flick with her husband.